Legends from the Pacific: Book 1

Kamuela Kaneshiro

Legends from the Pacific LLC

Contents

This book contains original stories from episode 1–50 of the "Legends from the Pacific" podcast.
While time, different cultures, and contradicting retellings altered many of these oral tales. My team and I meticulously researched these legends. I also treated these fables and their cultures with the utmost respect while writing our original stories. I hope you and future generations enjoy our original stories, and my writing is close to the version spoken centuries ago.
- Kamuela Kaneshiro

To hear our latest stories, listen to:
    Legends from the Pacific
The Asian & Pacific folklore, and cultural history podcast.
    www.LegendsFromThePacific.com

Introduction

"I felt Asian and Pacific cultural stories were being given the bad 80s movie treatment, and no one knew or cared."

I began working on film and television projects in the late 90s. Cast and crew asked me to share stories about my culture. So, I recalled childhood stories and discovered most of Hawaii's locals and Native Hawaiians weren't familiar with Hawaiian culture.

November 2004, before podcasting was a term, my friend Kenneth "Kento" Komoto, a professional comedian, and I started "Off the Air's: Geek Nation", a weekly 3-hour geek culture show. Geek Nation became a hybrid AM Radio/internet show. But after a few years, Kento understandably got burned out, and we stopped Geek Nation.

While productions continued asking about my culture. Movies, shows, streaming programs and the internet presented reworked cultural tales. While they were entertaining, many viewers didn't know the presented material was far from the original story, or aware an original story existed.

The 80s had terrible movies so loosely based on popular intellectual property (IP) that the films only shared the main character's name, and sometimes the IP title.

I felt Asian and Pacific cultural stories were being given the bad 80s movie treatment, and no one knew or cared.

However, bad 80s movies were not the only culprits. Various factors, including time-blurred memories and storytellers, who accidentally or deliberately stripped away story elements, caused tales to become fractured shadows of their original versions.

To restore these stories, I began researching, and started the podcast "Legends from the Pacific" in February 2020.

While it's impossible to get everything right, and sadly, even if a story's original creator appeared, they'd probably be mocked and criticized. It's my hope our stories are close to their original versions.

Mahalo nui loa for your support and thanks for reading my writing.

Kamuela Kaneshiro.

Elders vs. Scholars

The Hawaiian okina (') looks like a backward inverted apostrophe, but it's a consonant, treated as a pause like a music rest. The okina changes Hawaiian words, and while dictionaries and other reference material suggested certain words included an okina, Hawaiian elders disagreed.

This book follows the Hawaiian elder's recommended spellings.

PELE

HAWAI'I'S GODDESS OF FIRE

P ELE IS ONE OF Hawai'i's most active deities. It's customary to offer food, tobacco, and gin to gain her favor. She appears as a beautiful young maiden or an old woman asking for help, usually before her beloved Kilauea volcano erupts. Whoever helps Pele is spared from her devastating lava.

Those who take her volcanic rocks are plagued by misfortune. This is Pele's curse, which is lifted when the souvenirs are returned. People who ignored the curse often mail their rocks back to the Big Island along with an apology letter detailing their misfortune and where to replace the rock.

Pele wanders through all the islands, sometimes with her big white dog. They frequent Oahu's Pali Highway, where it is forbidden to travel with pork. Motorists with pork have experienced misfortune and car problems. When the pork is removed, their vehicles resume functioning.

Pele's sister is the ocean goddess Namaka. Before Pele was a goddess, she lived in Tahiti and seduced Namaka's husband. When Namaka found out, Pele fled Tahiti and created land to protect her from Namaka. This is one story of how the Hawaiian Islands were created.

ORIGINS
Inspired by folklore

In the beginning, there was the Pacific Ocean. A canoe broke the horizon, piloted by Pele, a beautiful Polynesian maiden who dominated the waves until she felt safe to stop. Pele used a digging stick given to her by her uncle to make a pit of molten lava that was cooled by the sea and became an island.

The ocean goddess's eyes narrowed as she towered over Pele, her sister who seduced her husband. The goddess defeated Pele, extinguished the firepit, and left her sister for dead.

But the hotheaded maiden forced her battered body into her canoe and sailed east. The sisters fought several more times on Pele's new islands until the goddess killed her adulterous sister.

Pele's soul flickered, and she became the goddess of fire.

During a present-day Hawaiian luau, a tourist looking for the smoking section encountered a Polynesian maiden. He offered her a cigarette. She accepted and lit it with fire from her finger.

THE SUGARCANE FIELD
Inspired by folklore

One night while driving through Oahu's North Shore sugarcane fields, a man hit a woman in a white dress. He slammed on his brakes. Her folded body remained on the hood of his car. As he tried figuring out where the woman came from, she lifted her head, smiled, and floated into the sky.

PELE'S DOG AT THE PALI
Inspired by collected testimony

When I was younger, my friends and I were in my friend's truck going over the Pali from town to Kailua. I was riding in the bed with others, and the clouds were low like fog, which was strange because Hawai'i doesn't really have fog.

While the fog streamed around the truck, I noticed a white cloud in the middle of the road. The cloud was following us. I thought it was the moon or light reflected from the truck. But the cloud was getting bigger and closer. Then I realized the cloud was a big white dog.

My friends also saw it.

"Pele's dog is chasing us," a friend yelled to the others riding inside.

The driver gunned it. We pulled away as the dog returned to the fog.

We were scared because we saw Pele's dog, so she must be around. But we didn't see her.

THE HITCHHIKING GHOST
Inspired by collected testimony

Decades ago, on the Big Island of Hawai'i, a man drove home from his graveyard shift. The inconsistent hours and taking the kids to school or whatever they were doing blurred his days. He rubbed his face and struggled, keeping his tired eyes focused on the desolate road.

His unbuckled seat belt clicked against the door.

Smoking kept him awake, but his two remaining cigarettes wouldn't cover the trip. He should have fixed his broken radio, but that money went to his family. Even if he had a radio, it'd probably just catch static. But static might keep him awake.

Something along the road caught his eye. An old Hawaiian lady hobbled on the shoulder. Her white dress reflected his headlights as he pulled over.

"Eh, you need a ride?"

"Yes," the woman said. "Mahalo."

He unlocked the passenger door. But the woman went to the back door. He unlocked it, and she opened it with a smile.

"You can sit in the front," he said.

"No, I'm fine." The woman settled in and closed the door.

He nodded and pulled back onto the grim road.

He offered her a cigarette. She accepted it, and he took his last one. He offered her his lighter.

She waved it away. "'*A'ole pilikia*. No problem." The lady held her finger to the cigarette. A flame appeared on her fingertip, and she lit her cigarette.

The man lit his. *I must be tired.*

The lady's silhouette dominated his rearview mirror. Her cigarette illuminated her face when she took a draw. Then the darkness reclaimed her.

He cleared his throat. "Where do you live? I don't mind taking you home."

Smoke loomed around her.

His unbuckled seat belt clicked against his door.

She faced Kilauea, silhouetted against the predawn horizon. "The volcano looks strange."

He chuckled. "The volcano is dormant. It hasn't erupted in years."

"The volcano looks strange." She faced the rearview mirror. "You need to place ti leaves around your house. Do that. Okay?"

"Okay? Hey, what was your name?"

The shadows claimed the lady and her glowing cigarette.

The man slammed the brakes. His back seat was empty. He left his car and scanned the deserted road. "Pele," he whispered. He jumped back into his car and sped home. His family didn't believe him and worried he needed to sleep more.

Days later, Kilauea volcano erupted. Lava rivers destroyed roads, reclaimed the developed land, and threatened residential areas. Many evacuated, some stayed and cried while lava consumed their homes. Amid this, a lava stream split in half and avoided a house surrounded by Hawaiian ti leaves.

DR. GLEN GRANT

HAWAI'I'S GHOST MAN

D R. GLEN GRANT WAS from Los Angeles, California. His father, Cliff Grant, worked on special effects for many famous Hollywood films. Dr. Grant smiled when telling me about his dad and times when he and his siblings were allowed to play with the flying monkey masks used in the *Wizard of Oz*. Dr. Grant proudly displayed a miniature cannon used in *20,000 Leagues under the Sea* and talked about his brother Robby the Robot from the film *The Forbidden Planet*, who'd make cameos in other science fiction productions.

Dr. Grant received his master's in education from the University of Hawai'i and a doctorate in American studies. He taught at UH and the Hawai'i Tokai International University, where he also served as vice chancellor.

Dr. Grant collected Hawaiian and Asian ghost stories and took people on ghost tours. His company was called Chicken Skin, which is Hawaiian pidgin, or local slang, for goose bumps. He wrote several books, including *The Obake Files*, and had a weekly radio show, *Chicken Skin Radio*.

Because of Dr. Grant's passion for Hawai'i's supernatural stories, people called him the Obake man. Obake is Japanese slang for ghost. He opened a coffee shop, the Haunt, where he began his tours. But while Dr. Grant took people on bus tours to haunted areas or guided them through graveyards in the middle of the night, he'd be the first to admit that he was the world's biggest chicken and he hated when people on his tour would see something behind him.

He'd see the group's eyes widen and wait for him to finish his story.

One would point behind him. "Dr. Grant, what's that?"

Dr. Grant dreaded turning around, and if something was there, he'd be the first to run for their bus.

Dr. Grant passed from cancer. His business partner, Jill, experienced a lot of challenges. I helped her with the Haunt and was honored to host Mōʻiliʻili's annual storytelling night, which Dr. Grant normally did.

Jill closed the Haunt after a falling-out with associates, and others registered Dr. Grant's Chicken Skin business name.

Jill, the ghost hunters, and I miss Dr. Grant. We conducted a séance but got nothing. We still hope he is at peace.

THE GRAVEYARD
Inspired by a true story

On a clear night, Dr. Grant took a few people to a graveyard. As the moon emerged from the clouds, a shimmering, elongated apparition drifted between the graves. Everyone screamed, piled into their car, and sped to town.

They calmed down and talked about how something seemed off about what they'd seen. They returned to the graveyard, found the shimmering form, and approached. It was water from a sprinkler, reflecting the streetlights or moon.

DR. GRANT, THE GHOST HUNTERS, AND I
Based on true events

The coffee shop's creaking door was something from a haunted house. It announced my arrival to people at the tables on the left while others pursued the bookshelves on my right. A posted menu advertised drinks, snacks, and this Saturday's dinner and a movie. Beside it, Dr. Glen Grant leaned on the countertop, waved to me, and resumed listening to his customer.

I closed the door as the customer ended his story.

Dr. Grant stood. "See, what I'd like to do is make a group. A ghost hunter society people and businesses could call to investigate their disturbances."

I approached. "If you create such a group, I'll be the first to sign up."

He smiled. "Neat."

We talked, and he was impressed I was a magician with a background in film, a member of the American Society for Psychical Research, and that I conducted my own investigations.

I became a regular on his radio show, where he introduced me as the embodiment of the *Obake Files*. Obake is Japanese slang for ghost.

We formed the Hawai'i Ghost Hunters Society and helped residents and businesses with their paranormal problems. The Society unofficially met at Dr. Grant's Haunt during its Saturday-night dinner-and-a-movie events.

Dr. Grant had others do his bus tours, so we'd watch the tour leave, discuss our next investigation over dinner, and enjoy an old movie. We had about two dozen members. I ensured some were skeptics, but toward the end, everyone had a few unexplainable incidents.

During our official Society meetings, Dr. Grant briefed us about our case and included the location's history. He joined us a couple of times but avoided fieldwork.

When Dr. Grant passed from cancer, we had a few cases, but things were difficult because people couldn't contact us, and we spent a lot of time researching locations. The Society was disbanded.

Dr. Grant once asked if I'd be interested in doing tours for him. I was honored but politely declined, and he understood that someone needed to investigate the stories and experiences.

DR. GRANT & THE PALI
Inspired by a true story

It had been a while since Dr. Grant did his Pali Highway bus tour, but he soldiered on with his stories. As the bus pulled onto Pali Road, Dr. Grant's guests were leaning forward in their seats, listening to his story.

Banging ran across the top of the bus.

Dr. Grant screamed and dove into his front seat.

The banging was low-hanging vines thumping along the bus.

THE MONSTER AND DEMON OF CHINESE NEW YEAR

THE MONSTER
Inspired by folklore

THE EXPIRING DAY'S LONG shadows added fear to the panicked villagers. They were supposed to be in the mountains by now. Urgency hastened their packing, and fussy children worked on everyone's last nerve.

An old beggar entered the chaotic village, but his request for food and water fell on deaf ears.

The village elder took in the beggar and fed him.

"Why is everyone packing?" the beggar said. "It's the new year. They should be celebrating."

The elder lowered her head. "The night's new moon brings a monster from the sea. It attacks our village and devours anyone it grabs."

The beggar nodded. "For the hospitality you've shown me, I'll rid you of your monster."

"No, I didn't ask for this. It will kill you. Join us in the mountains."

"Thank you, but I'll be fine. You be with your people. I must stay and prepare."

The night brought the new moon and the monster from the sea. The creature scurried into the village. A dwelling adorned in red paper made the monster rear back.

The beggar emerged from the dwelling, dressed in red, making as much noise as he could.

The ruckus assaulted the monster's senses. It thrashed and struggled to flee.

The beggar lit fireworks.

The explosions startled the creature, and it scrambled away.

The beggar laughed as he lost sight of the monster. The villagers returned and thanked him for saving their village.

Ever since, on Chinese New Year, people wear red, hang red paper on houses, and light fireworks to ensure a good year.

THE LANTERN FESTIVAL
Inspired by folklore

In times past, a sacred bird materialized in our realm. Hunters, unaware the bird was from the heavenly plane, killed it. This infuriated the Jade Emperor, who ordered the gods to burn our realm.

But the gods didn't agree with the Jade Emperor and told the villagers of his plan.

People hung red lanterns to trick the Jade Emperor into believing their villages were on fire.

When the Jade Emperor looked down on our realm, he believed the red lanterns were flames consuming everything, and he was pleased.

THE CHINESE ZODIAC
Inspired by folklore

The Jade Emperor created a long-distance race for the world's animals. The first twelve to finish would be honored with its own year.

The rat was clever and tricked his friend the cat into thinking the race was the next day. The cat napped to prepare for the race while the rat began the contest.

The rat encountered an ox who started early because he knew the journey would be difficult.

The rat waved to the ox. "Your legs are more suited for this race than mine. Can you please carry me?"

The ox agreed.

The rat rode the ox, motivating him to go faster.

As they neared the finish line, the rat jumped from the ox and claimed first place.

The ox took second.

The cat missed the race.

This is why cats are not in the Chinese zodiac and are enemies of rats.

THE DEMON
Inspired by folklore

Parents stay up at night to protect their children from a demon. If the demon taps a child's head three times, a fever will develop. If the child survives, they will suffer mental trauma.

A mother illuminated her son's cold room with a fresh candle. She smiled as she passed her husband sitting in a chair. She closed the window beside her son's bed and placed the fragile light on the stand beside him.

Their son fidgeted in bed.

His father suggested their son needed something to tire him and gave him several shiny coins.

His mother provided red paper and told him to wrap the coins, open them, and repeat the process.

The candle burned low. Drowsiness tugged the parents' heads.

The father woke.

His son slept in bed.

Embarrassment burned the father's cheeks. *I should be a better father and stay awake for my son.*

Something moved beyond the open window. It was the demon, and it peeked into the room.

The father tried to stand, but he was paralyzed.

The demon blew out the candle. Darkness filled the room.

The father's eyes adjusted.

The demon's tail flicked as its wings filled the room. Its yellow eyes and white teeth pierced the dark as it approached the sleeping child.

The father struggled against his unresponsive body.

The demon licked its lips and raised a fist over the child.

The father tried screaming. Silence remained.

The demon's knuckle tapped the boy's head three times.

The father's heart sank. Tears welled up. But his paralysis was broken. He lunged at the demon.

The fiend laughed and leaped for the window.

Its tail slid across the father's palm. His fingers curled around the tail.

His son coughed.

He faced his child. The demon's tail slipped through his fingers, and the fiend flew out the window.

The father cradled his son. He burned with a fever.

The father cried, begging his son to fight the sickness.

A hand grabbed the father's shoulder. He woke to his smiling wife.

The room was lit. The window was closed, and his son slept in bed beside a low-burning candle.

"You had a nightmare," his wife said. "Go to sleep. You had a long day and have to work in the morning."

He shook his head. "I just need to wash my face."

The mother checked on their son. The dissolving candle extinguished. The red paper beside her child's head glowed in the faint ambient light, and the coins reflected her image.

The room brightened. Her husband entered with a lantern and replaced the candles.

Something fell in the outer room.

The parents exchanged glances and left.

The demon opened the window, blew out the fresh candle, and approached the sleeping child.

The parents' footsteps approached.

The demon made a fist, but the red paper beside the child scared it, and the coins reflected the monster's image.

The fiend recoiled.

Mother and father rushed into the room.

The demon cowered in the corner, hissed, then flew out the window.

Ever since, it has been customary to give children money wrapped in red paper to keep demons away and encourage good luck.

BUNYIP
THE ABORIGINAL WATER DEVIL

B UNYIP MEANS *DEVIL* OR *evil spirit*, but these monsters are also called dongu, yaa-loo, and wowee-wowee. They appear as a seal, hippopotamus, or reptile, with claws and feathers. They have magical abilities and dwell in watering holes, eating animals or humans who get too close.

Aboriginals believe the bunyip was a man from their time of creation who ate his totem animal, breaking the Rainbow Serpent's law.

THE OUTLINE
Inspired by folklore

A hunting party knew a creature inhabited the watering hole, but the oasis beckoned them from the barren outback. At the bank, something pounced from the water and ate a hunter. The others woke from their shock and killed the creature.

They dragged the creature's twenty-eight-foot-long body ashore, traced its outline on the ground, and named it bunyip.

Their descendants maintained the outline. George Henry Wathen mentioned it in his 1855 book, *The Golden Colony,* and R. E. Johns sketched it in 1867. But the land was cultivated, which destroyed the outline.

THE STOLEN BABY
Inspired by folklore

When the outback provided less, the tribe's hunters set traps farther from their village, which caught a small bunyip beside a watering hole.

They had never seen a bunyip before, and it made a peculiar sound. The water behind them stirred, and they realized the baby was calling its mother.

The mother bunyip lunged for the hunters but missed.

They grabbed the infant, which cried as it was taken from its home.

The tribe welcomed their hunters and prepared to eat the baby and capture its mother.

But bunyips are magical, and the mother, with members of her pack, created a tidal wave that slammed the village. The enchanted water turned the villagers into swans. Those who avoided the water were eaten by bunyips, and the baby was reunited with its mother.

LIMA'S LA CASA MATUSITA

L A CASA MATUSITA, OR the house of Matusita, is one of Lima's most haunted places. Many believe the area was cursed in the 1700s by Dervaspa Parvaneh, a Persian healer who practiced alternative medicine. The Spanish Inquisition persecuted and tortured her until she confessed to being a witch. They burned her at the stake, but she cursed the area before she died.

A wealthy man who built his house on the cursed site met a gruesome end. A Japanese family, the Matsushitas, whom the house is named after, moved in and met a tragic end.

More deaths and unusual phenomena followed. But some believe the house isn't haunted and spirits of deceased prisoners from the nearby jail caused the activity. Others claim the stories were fabricated because the house was an ideal location to spy on the old US Embassy.

THE FIRST OWNER
Inspired by folklore

Mistreated servants planned on getting even with their master by spiking the drinks of his next feast. They greeted the guests, drugged the beverages with a hallucinogenic powder, left, and listened behind locked doors.

The rambunctious party softened. Screams erupted amid the sound of breaking plates. The servants scrambled to unlock the doors, but most of the noise stopped when they were opened.

Blood lined the walls and dripped from the tables. A few pale guests sat while some fought each other and the rest bled out on the floor. Their master was an eviscerated, limbless mass.

The servants were admitted into an asylum but never recovered.

THE MATSUSHITAS
Inspired by folklore

The Matsushitas immigrated from Japan to Peru and moved into the two-story building. The husband ran a store downstairs while his family lived above it.

One day he came home early from an errand. He looked forward to surprising his children when they came home from school but found his wife with another man. The husband grabbed a kitchen knife and killed the lovers.

Their blood soaked the bed and lined the walls.

His children thumped up the staircase and encountered their distressed father.

He killed them with his kitchen knife, then killed himself.

THE EXORCIST
Inspired by folklore

A shopkeeper running a downstairs store requested the church do something about annoying noises upstairs.

The sounds intensified in the following weeks, then settled when he began eating lunch.

The shop's door opened, but shelves blocked the customer.

"Hello," the shopkeeper said. "How may I help you?"

The customer approached. "I am not here to buy anything," a raspy voice wheezed.

The shopkeeper frowned. "Why'd you come in?"

"I was sent for." A panting elderly man emerged from the aisle. He carried a black bag and adjusted his priestly collar.

"I'm sorry, Father. Would you like some water?"

The priest nodded and wiped his brow with his handkerchief.

The shopkeeper gave him water. "I'm sorry, I didn't expect you."

The priest sipped his water. "It's our understanding you have experienced some disturbances?"

"Yes. Upstairs."

"Has your family experienced this?"

"No."

"Has the family living there experienced this?"

"Family? The upstairs is abandoned. Have you read my request?"

The priest smirked. "We receive many claims of this nature. I'm being thorough. You have the upstairs keys?"

"Yes. You don't want to rest?"

"No, thank you. Let's go." He collected his black bag.

The shopkeeper grabbed a flashlight and took the priest to the door.

"I've never seen an exorcism before," the shopkeeper said.

The priest nodded. "It's become second nature for me. You'll have nothing to fear."

"Oh, I never go upstairs."

The priest faced him.

The shopkeeper paled. "I must watch my store." He opened the door, revealing a dim staircase. "Did you need someone to assist you?"

The priest swallowed. "No, I'll be fine."

"Thank you, Father." The shopkeeper handed him the flashlight and closed the door, plunging the priest into darkness.

The priest wheezed as he turned on the flashlight. The afternoon-baked walls made him wish he was outside. He flicked the light switch.

The click echoed.

He sighed, wiped his face with his handkerchief, and kept it out as he went upstairs.

Sweat dripped from the drenched handkerchief as he gasped on the stagnant second-floor air. Light bled between the boards nailed across the windows, and dust carpeted the floor.

"Is anyone here?" he wheezed.

Shadows moved in the corners. Beady eyes reflected in his flashlight's beam.

Rats. He placed his bag on the floor. Silence throbbed his ears.

Something grabbed his hair.

He swatted at it but hit nothing.

Something touched the back of his neck.

He spun around and faced the stairs. He prayed.

Something whispered in his ears.

His scream echoed in the neighborhood.

Silence returned.

The downstairs door opened. The shopkeeper glanced upstairs. "Father? Are you all right?" The flashlight was beside the bottom stair. He picked it up, tried turning it on, but it didn't work. "Father?" He swung the door open.

Light filled the stairs.

He crept up them. "Father?"

The priest's bag lay on the floor.

"Hello?" a man said from the downstairs door.

The shopkeeper turned toward him, but his eyes remained on the room's open doors. "Hello."

"I heard a scream. Is everything all right?"

The shopkeeper's hand shook. "Please come here. A priest is here. I think something happened to him."

"A priest?" Heavy footsteps ran up the stairs.

A young man joined the shopkeeper's side and scanned the room. "Where's the priest?"

The shopkeeper shook his head and shrugged.

"Let's check the other rooms." The young man ran to a room. "Father? Are you here?"

The shopkeeper approached a room but returned to the stairs.

The young man found the priest's dead body in what might have been the master bedroom. They say he died from a heart attack. The shopkeeper continued his business until he had enough of the noises upstairs.

PASADENA'S COLORADO STREET BRIDGE

THE 1,486-FOOT-LONG BRIDGE OPENED in 1913. It's 150 feet high and part of Route 66. Its first death occurred during its construction when an accident claimed a worker who was entombed.

Six years later, in 1919, the first suicide occurred. More followed during the Great Depression. They nicknamed the bridge the Suicide Bridge, which businesses used in ads.

The bridge's apparitions include a man with wire glasses and screaming ghosts who leap from the bridge. While under the bridge, witnesses reported cold spots, disembodied voices, and a change in animals' behavior.

A MOTHER'S CLARITY
Inspired by a true story

The California sun rose as a mother took her three-year-old daughter from their car onto the bridge.

Almost ten years had passed since the stock market's Black Tuesday caused people to snap. My husband snapped like the rest of them. That's why he left us. But it didn't matter because I was answering a calling.

Wind teared my tired eyes as I peered over the side.

The bottom seemed so close, but that's why it held the answer.

Something moved at the edge of my peripheral. I clutched my daughter and faced it.

A man with wire-rim spectacles approached.

I sighed. "You sure gave me a fright, mister. I didn't hear you." Guilt hardened in my stomach. I glanced between my daughter and the railing. "We were, um, just enjoying the sunrise."

He passed.

I chuckled. Lord, this was crazy. What was I going to do if that man hadn't interrupted me?

I wiped a tear. "Hey, mister. Can you help me? I lost my job, and I don't think I'm right."

No one was with us.

My skin prickled. I had snapped like the rest of them. The sun irritated my eyes, and the bottom called to me. I took my daughter into an alcove, tossed her over, and jumped after her.

Story Notes:

The mother passed, but her daughter survived.

A QUICK RUN
Inspired by folklore

The bridge was so lovely I included it in my evening run. It was dark before I knew it, but there was something on one of the parapets. It was a lady in a dress. Somehow I knew she was going to jump, and she did.

I screamed and raced to the railing, but she vanished. I'm sure that run home was a personal best.

HER FAULT
Inspired by folklore

A homeless man enjoyed the sunset with his scrawny dog. He loved California's weather and laughed. *They're probably freezing their butts off back in Chicago.* He wandered the night with his dog and approached the foot of a gorgeous bridge. *Hope no one throws anything over.* His dog wasn't panting beside him but several feet behind.

"Come on, Charlie. Stay close."

Charlie's ears fell as he took his side, and they approached a homeless encampment.

"Hello?" one of the group said.

"Hello." The man smiled. "It's just me an' my dog. We don't want no trouble, just a place for the night. Maybe longer?"

The clustered mass stirred.

"You folks mind?"

"No animals," a voice said.

"Charlie?" He chuckled. "He'd never hurt a fly."

Charlie gave his tail a wag.

"That's the rules. You can stay but not the dog."

The man petted Charlie. "It's okay, you're a good boy." He studied the group, then a sprawling area in the bridge's shadow. *Funny they're not spread out.* He faced the group. "Look. There's more than enough space for us. What if we kept our distance?"

"Just keep that dog away and stay out of the shadow."

The man chuckled. "All right. Me and Charlie will take this whole area, and you stay huddled up there."

The homeless group shook their heads as the man and Charlie went toward the dark.

"The nerve of those guys," he said, entering the darkness. "What makes them think they're better than us? Right, Charlie?"

Pebbles shifted under him. Charlie wasn't beside him.

"Charlie?" He spun around.

Charlie stood at the edge of the light. A growl rumbled, and his reflecting eyes were locked on the man.

"Charlie, come here."

Charlie snarled. Drool dripped from his white teeth as his fur bristled along his spine.

"Come on, boy—"

Barking erupted from the dog's snapping jaws.

A chill prickled the man's skin.

Charlie whimpered.

Something loomed behind the man. "Her fault," a guttural moan whispered.

The man spun around and swung.

Nothing was there.

"Her fault," the guttural voice said.

The man ran from the darkness.

"Her fault," echoed behind him.

Charlie whined and joined his master, running into the night.

RANGDA
BALI'S QUEEN OF DEMONS

R ANGDA IS OLD JAVANESE for *widow* but is also the name of a witch or the queen of demons. Rangda the witch lives in the jungle and commands leyaks, or demons.

Leyaks commonly appear as people during the day, but at night their heads sprout wings and fly from their bodies with their organs attached.

Rangda and Leyaks enjoy hunting and eating children or pregnant women. But some people in Bali see Rangda as a protective being similar to the Hindu goddess Kali. Rangda and Kali also share similar iconography, colors, and are both depicted with protruding tongues. Popular Rangda masks portray the goddess with budging eyes, fangs, and a long tongue.

The historic figure Princess Mahendradatta has been compared with Rangda. She was a powerful and feared woman who practiced witchcraft in the late tenth century. She married an unknown person and had a son, Airlangga.

It's unknown what happened to her husband, but she's considered a widow, Rangda. Mahendradatta married King Udayana, who exiled her into the jungle after discovering she promoted the Hindu goddess of war, Durga.

Mahendradatta inspired the character Calon Arang. Calon Arang was a witch who lived in the jungle with her beautiful daughter. But the village men ignored her daughter because they wanted nothing to do with Calon Arang.

Modern interpretations illustrate Calon Arang as a victim of patriarchy.

THE JUNGLE WITCH
Inspired by folklore

Two children hurried home along a familiar path as night changed the jungle from dangerous to deadly.

One stopped and waved at the trees. "Someone's up there. They can help us get home."

A man's face peeked from behind the treetop's branches.

They called him.

His head rose from the branches. It didn't have a body.

The children screamed and raced home.

The disembodied head flew to a cackling woman mocking the screaming children. Her long nails petted the head, her white fangs matched her eyes, and her long tongue almost touched the ground as she hunched forward, pursuing the children.

A MOTHER'S LOVE
Inspired by folklore

Calon Arang's heartbroken teenage daughter ran home. Tears blurred her vision. "All I want is a husband," she wailed.

Her mother knew they had rejected her daughter again. She comforted her beautiful child till she cried herself to sleep.

I'm sorry they punish you because of me, the witch. She kissed her daughter's head. Calon Arang's eyes glowed as she consulted her spell book and became a specter in the night.

A teenage girl wandered from the village and called for her lover.

Calon Arang collected her.

The teen begged to be released.

The mother only heard her daughter's crying. Her eyes glowed.

The girl whimpered.

Calon Arang consulted her book and began the ritual.

The air shimmered.

She completed the ritual, and a portal appeared.

The Hindu goddess of war, Durga, stepped into our realm.

Calon Arang bowed.

Durga approached the sobbing teen and guided her into the realm of death.

The goddess faced the witch. "Your offer is acceptable. What do you request?"

Calon Arang clenched her fists. A tear fell from her eye. "Mistress Durga, the villagers mistreat my daughter. Unleash a flood and plague upon them for their treachery."

Durga's eyes glowed. She nodded and disappeared.

Calon Arang's eyes dimmed. She closed her book, and the mother sobbed.

Durga ravished the lands with flood and plague. The king learned of Calon Arang's vengeance and ordered his mystic adviser, Empu Bharada, to handle the witch.

Empu Bharada learned the witch was displeased because no men accepted her beautiful daughter and tasked a disciple to marry her.

The disciple agreed.

Calon Arang held a seven-day feast and reveled in her daughter's joy.

After the feast, the disciple found Calon's spell book. He learned it was the source of her power and took it to his master.

The king sent Empu Bharada with an army to kill her.

The disciple took them to the witch's house.

Empu Bharada ordered the army not to attack as they surrounded the home. He called to Calon Arang.

Mother and daughter exited her hut.

"I am Empu Bharada. I have your book and know you're weakened without it. Please change your ways and become a lawful member of our land."

Calon Arang's daughter faced her. "Mother?"

"Hush, child." Calon Arang stepped away and faced the mystic. "Your dealings are with me, the witch. Not my daughter."

Empu Bharada stepped forward. "Please don't do this. Consider your daughter."

The mother laughed. "You're blind if you can't see I haven't."

Empu Bharada bit his lip.

Calon Arang pointed at him. "You'd accept me. Not others, like your king."

Empu Bharada nodded to his army. Nearby, soldiers dragged Calon Arang's daughter away.

She protested and screamed at her mother.

Calon Arang's eyes watered. She funneled her grief into a cackle. "I'd rather die as I am than conform to your misguided standards."

She attacked.

Empu Bharada made her death quick and painless.

Her daughter grieved. Her husband comforted her. She understood her mother's sacrifice and began her life, crafted by her mother.

BABA YAGA
RUSSIA'S BOGEYMAN

Baba Yaga is a powerful witch, keeper of mystic items, and summoner of several disembodied flying hands to do her bidding. She flies in a giant mortar and sweeps her tracks away with a broom. Her house walks on chicken legs and is entered by saying, "Turn your back to the woods and your front to me."

Baba is short for Babushka, Russian for grandmother, sorcerer, or fortune-teller. Yaga is a negative term with no direct meaning.

She's depicted as an individual or three separate women, similar to Macbeth's Weird Sisters. She appears as a worn-out hag who sharpens her teeth to eat children.

Baba Yaga can smell nearby Russians and has traveled with three horsemen, representing the day, sun, and night, which symbolizes her control over natural elements.

She has many human and supernatural children, who may include the devil.

Baba Yaga's a villain who's assisted heroes, and while she's died in stories, she always returns.

BABA YAGA & VASILISA
Inspired by folklore

A merchant and his wife had a daughter named Vasilisa. When Vasilisa was eight, her mother became bedridden.

She gave Vasilisa a wooden doll. "My dear Vasilisa, when you are in need, give the doll a little to drink and a little to eat."

Vasilisa's mother died.

The child gave her doll a little to drink and a little to eat, and the doll comforted her.

Years later, Vasilisa's father married a woman with two daughters. Vasilisa's stepmother loved the fine things her merchant husband provided but despised Vasilisa. She spoiled her daughters and made Vasilisa do all the chores.

Vasilisa obeyed because she honored her stepmother and saw how happy her father was. She completed whatever was asked of her with help from her doll.

When Vasilisa's father needed to leave for several days for business, her stepmother learned Baba Yaga lived in the nearby woods.

When he left, the stepmother moved the family to a hut beside Baba Yaga's forest and sent Vasilisa to get fire from Baba Yaga.

She followed a path. Shadows moved in the canopied woods, and the keening wind prickled Vasilisa's skin. A galloping horse behind her approached. A white rider and steed passed.

Something glowed in the clearing. A galloping horse behind her approached. A red rider and steed passed.

The clearing's light was from glowing skulls on fence posts surrounding a house with chicken legs.

A galloping horse behind her approached. A black rider and steed passed.

Vasilisa approached the house. Coals in the skulls made them glow.

Baba Yaga's mortar erupted from the path.

The witch cackled and peered over the mortar's rim. "Little girl, what are you doing outside my house?"

Vasilisa bowed. "Grandmother, my family moved into a cottage outside your woods. We don't have fire. Can you please give us some?"

Baba Yaga landed beside Vasilisa and studied her. "You honor me by calling me Grandmother, but my fire is precious. What will you trade?"

"Trade?" Vasilisa had the clothes she was wearing and her doll. "I have nothing to offer, Grandmother. If you could please loan us—"

"I'll do nothing of the sort, little girl." Baba Yaga grinned. "I'll give you fire if you live with me for three days and complete my chores. But if you fail, I get to eat you. Do you agree, my child?"

The witch's eyes reflected Vasilisa's face.

"I agree, Grandmother."

Baba Yaga's cackle echoed throughout the woods. She commanded her house to lower and welcomed Vasilisa into her domain.

Baba Yaga made dinner, sat at the table, and pointed at the ground. Vasilisa sat where the witch pointed. Baba Yaga sloppily devoured her food and tossed Vasilisa a few scraps.

The child didn't eat but listened as Baba Yaga listed a week's worth of chores.

The witch stood. "Sleep on the floor, little girl. Remember, if you leave, I'll find and eat you." She flopped into bed and dreamed of eating Vasilisa.

Fear shrank Vasilisa's appetite, and she gave her doll a little to drink and a little to eat.

"My dear Vasilisa," the doll said. "Do not fear Baba Yaga for I will help you. Now please go to sleep, for morning is wiser than evening."

The following day, Baba Yaga reminded Vasilisa of her chores and flew off in her mortar, cackling.

Vasilisa and her doll spent the day completing the chores, and the white rider galloped past.

"My dear Vasilisa," her doll said. "Baba Yaga will soon arrive. Please keep your wits. She enjoys keeping dark secrets and may kill you for asking too many questions."

The red rider galloped past.

Vasilisa thanked her doll and pocketed it as the black rider galloped past.

Baba Yaga flew in from the woods and jumped from her mortar.

Vasilisa completed all her tasks, and the witch screamed.

Baba Yaga searched for flaws. She summoned several disembodied hands, gave them an order, and they vanished. The witch entered her house, mumbling about Vasilisa's success.

At dinner, Baba Yaga scowled from behind her food as Vasilisa ate her scraps.

"You barely talk for a little girl."

"I didn't feel I could."

Baba Yaga grinned. "You may always talk, child. But too many questions can be deadly."

Vasilisa looked up from her scraps. "The riders, who are they, and why are they white, red, and black?"

"They are my glorious day, bright sun, and dark night. Anything else, child?"

A question about the disembodied hands rose in Vasilisa.

Baba Yaga's eyes gleamed. "What other questions do you have?"

Vasilisa faced her scraps. "Nothing, Grandmother. That's all I wanted to know."

Baba Yaga thumped the table. "Curse you, child. I almost had you. How can a feeble little girl complete a week of chores in one day and outwit me?"

Vasilisa glanced from her scraps. "I have my mother's blessing."

Baba Yaga gasped and toppled over her chair. She crawled to her feet and dragged Vasilisa outside.

"Grandmother, what's going on?"

"Why of all, a blessing from one's mother?" Baba Yaga snatched a glowing skull, checked its burning coals, put it on a stick, and gave it to Vasilisa. "There, take it and leave. You're not welcome here anymore." The witch stormed into her home.

Vasilisa used the light beaming from the skull's eyes to find the path home. She emerged from the woods, but her house was dark.

Her stepmother and stepsisters yelled how they couldn't make fire.

Vasilisa opened the door.

Their yelling stopped.

"Vasilisa?" her stepmother said. "What are you holding? Is it from Baba Yaga?"

"Yes, it's light and fire."

Vasilisa displayed the glowing skull.

Its light beams fell upon the stepmother and sisters. They burst into flames, became piles of ash, and blew away.

Vasilisa screamed. She ran outside, buried the glowing skull, and cried.

"Hello?" a man said.

"Hello?" Vasilisa faced a man carrying a lantern.

He was part of the prince's procession who heard crying as they passed. The prince was infatuated with Vasilisa and reunited her with her father. Vasilisa became a wise, beautiful woman and married the prince.

EL CALEUCHE
CHILOTE'S PHANTOM SHIP

E L CALEUCHE IS A three-masted ghost ship crewed by the souls of drowned sailors or zombies. The ship sails off the coast of Chile and around the island of Chiloe.

El Caleuche is a living creature that vanishes when you get too close. It's older than the *Flying Dutchman* and other phantom ships. Many believe El Caleuche lures fishermen to join its crew, and supernatural beings like sorcerers or brujo use the ghost ship for traveling.

El Caleuche can sail underwater and is the only thing capable of reaching a great treasure. People who suddenly get rich are said to have made a pact, and El Caleuche delivered their wealth overnight.

THE NIGHT CRUISE
Inspired by folklore

You stumble from a bar and into the streets of Chiloe. You enjoy the inebriation of alcohol and being on vacation in this unique port city. Businesses close for the night, but you yearn to continue your adventure.

Music and laughter prick your ears. The festive sounds lead you to the waterfront and a party on a three-masted ship. The party's lights, dancing, and drinks entice you. You approach, passing buildings, which momentarily obstruct the party boat.

Emerging from the shadows, you look for the party boat's entrance, but the boat, music, and people are gone. Lights matching the party boat dance on the water, but you realize the lights are underwater, on the deck of the submerged party boat that sails out to sea.

ONE MAN'S DREAM
Inspired by folklore

A youngster gathered shellfish to sell at the market, where he encountered an elderly man asking for some seafood for his curanto. The young man offered the best of his collection.

The elder studied the shellfish. "My child, why is there no fish?"

The youngster chuckled. "I'll buy a boat when I have enough money, then I'll have fish."

The elder nodded, took some shellfish, and thanked the youngster, who ran to the market.

The youngster became a young man who sold shellfish at the market but always offered the elder the best of his collection.

"My young friend," the elder said. "Why is there no fish? You should have a boat now."

The young man smiled. "I met a girl. My money is going to her."

The elder nodded, took some shellfish, and thanked the young man, who strolled to the market.

The youngster became a graying man who sold shellfish at the market but always offered the elder the best of his collection.

"Your hair is graying," the elder said. "Why is there no fish? You should have a couple of boats now."

The man smirked. "The woman left me for a rich man. My money goes to distractions."

The elder nodded, took some shellfish, and thanked the graying man, who staggered to the market.

The graying man became an old man who sold shellfish at the market but always offered the elder the best of his collection.

"My friend," the elder said. "Why is there no fish? You should have a fleet."

The old man frowned. "My parents are sick. My money goes to caring for them."

The elder nodded, took some shellfish, and thanked the old man, who hobbled to the market.

The elder woke and found the old man sleeping beside his door.

The old man woke and bowed. "I'm sorry. I passed out here from a night of drinking." His eyes watered. "I worked hard and tried my best. But something always took my money whenever I had it. I'll never own a boat."

The elder pitied the old man, whom he still saw as a child.

"My friend," the elder whispered. "You work hard, but life is tricky. I am a brujo, and since you never hesitated giving me your best shellfish, I shall help you. Go home and rest."

The old man cried, thanked the brujo, and went home.

That night a three-masted ship delivered a fortune to the old man. He hired doctors who cured his parents. He purchased a fleet of ships and always supplied the brujo with fish.

OKIKU

THE SERVENT GIRL

O KIKU'S GHOST IS AN onryo, or vengeful spirit, that climbs from a well at night and begins counting. When the ghost reaches nine, she screams. If you hear her, you'll die soon. If she stops before nine, you'll live but may develop mental disorders.

This story began in the 1700s as a puppet theater, and her well is either at Japan's Himeji Castle or the Canadian Embassy. Many link this story with *The Ring* horror series.

THE GIRL IN THE WELL
Inspired by folklore

In old Japan, there was an attractive servant girl named Okiku who diligently guarded her master's treasures.

Her master desired her, but she rejected him.

To get his vengeance, he sneaked into his treasure room, took a decorative plate from his set of ten, and left.

Okiku noticed the missing plate. She counted them and confirmed there were only nine. She told her master and confessed she didn't know what happened.

"Don't cry, my dear Okiku," he said. "I'll forgive your carelessness if you became my lover."

Okiku paled. "I'm sorry, master. I don't think of you that way."

His eyes widened. He dragged Okiku outside and threw her into the palace well.

She died there, but her spirit haunts Japan.

THE LIVING DOLL

Hokkaido's Mannenji Temple has a doll that scientists confirmed has growing human hair. The doll was donated to the temple, but it's unclear if Okiku was the doll's name or that of its owner.

THE GIFT
Inspired by folklore

During the early 1900s, a child became sick while her brother was traveling. Around this time, he purchased a doll for his little sister and returned home. He was shocked to discover his sister was sick and gave her the doll.

She loved her gift, and the family did everything they could, but she died.

She was cremated, but her family forgot to include her beloved doll and added it to their home altar.

Time passed, and the doll's shoulder-length hair reached its waist. Believing their daughter's spirit was one with the doll, they cared for it and trimmed her hair when it grew out.

World War II forced the family to move. Worried about what may happen to the doll, they gave it to a temple to look after and explained its growing hair. The priests accepted the doll but thought nothing of it until its shoulder-length hair reached its waist.

KAMEHAMEHA THE GREAT

KAMEHAMEHA MEANS "THE VERY lonely one." Following the tradition that names were chants or statements, his full name was: Kalani Pai'ea Wohi o Kaleikini Keali'ikui Kamehameha o 'Iolani i Kaiwikapu kau'i Ka Liholiho Kunuiakea.

Referring to Kamehameha as Kam is considered disrespectful, since Kam doesn't sound like Kamehameha.

He was born around 1758 when Halley's Comet streaked across the storm-ridden Hawaiian Islands. Kahunas prophesied the unusual natural events signaled the birth of an exceptional individual.

Ali'i (Hawaiian chiefs) worried the prophesied individual would threaten their rule and ordered newborns killed. But Kamehameha was spirited to Hawai'i's Big Island and trained as a warrior.

It was prophesied that whoever overturned the five-thousand-pound Naha stone would unite the Hawaiian Islands. It is unknown how many times Kamehameha tried to overturn it, but he did at fourteen years old and gained support of some ali'i.

Around 1783, a twentysomething Kamehameha began his campaign to unite the islands. A critical supporter was Ka'ahumanu, a politically savvy Hawaiian who became Kamehameha's favorite wife and the Hawaiian Kingdom's most influential woman. Other supporters included British settlers Isaac Davis, John Young, Captain Brown, and ali'i like Kamuela Kaneshiro's ancestor, the Kaua'i chief Ka'iana, who was Kamehameha's most trusted adviser.

Hawaiian women were forbidden to become warriors but used firearms, which British and American traders supplied along with warships.

Captain James Cook met Kamehameha, but Kamehameha was not involved in Cook's death.

During Kamehameha's attempt to unite the Big Island, rival ali'i Keōua Kū'ahu'ula fled to Kilauea volcano, which erupted, endangering everyone. But Kamehameha cut a handful of hair and threw it into the lava, declaring himself to the goddess of fire Pele, and the eruption stopped. Kamehameha killed the ali'i and claimed the Big Island.

The islands of Maui, Lanai, and Molokai followed (elders stated these islands are not spelled with an okina [']). Kaho'olawe is uninhabited because it lacks water and resources. Control for O'ahu occurred in the 1790s with the Battle of Nu'uanu.

This famous battle was the bloodiest. Streams ran with blood, and the thirtysomething Kamehameha utilized the battlefield's Pali cliffs and pushed his enemies off. Because some jumped, Hawaiians called this battle Kaleleka'anae (leaping mullet).

The battle's death toll is unknown, but over one hundred years later, in 1898, construction workers found around eight hundred human skulls believed to be fallen warriors. This may add to the Nu'uanu area being one of Hawai'i's most haunted places.

With O'ahu, Kamehameha created the Hawaiian Kingdom.

Fifteen years later, in 1810, when Kamehameha was around forty-two, the remaining Hawaiian Islands Kaua'i and Ni'ihau joined, fulfilling Kamehameha's prophecy.

Kamehameha designed Hawai'i's flag with help from the Royal Hawaiian Navy, who were formerly with the British Royal Navy. Hawai'i's flag has eight stripes representing the Hawaiian Islands, with the United Kingdom's Union Flag in the corner.

In 1819, after ruling for nine years, Kamehameha was dying. Everyone wanted something from him, including his mana (power), stored in his bones. Kamehameha called his top advisers. Many took their time getting dressed, but two appeared as they were when they received his message. Kamehameha gave them the honor of hiding his remains.

They honored his wish, and the location of Kamehameha's body remains Hawai'i's greatest unsolved mystery.

A Hawaiian saying states, "Only the stars of the heavens know the resting place of Kamehameha." With him at peace, his death fulfilled his name, the Lonely One.

HAWAIIAN LANGUAGE

Though the Hawaiian language was only verbal, like with most Pacific cultures, the proper pronunciation for Hawaiian words is unknown because of regional dialects and altered records.

Hawai'i's history was taught through verbal stories and the hula. But much of Hawai'i's history was lost when missionaries banned the hula, and they produced a censored written form of Hawaiian language.

CAUCASIANS

Hawaiians were deeply spiritual, and the Caucasian's fair complexion made them seem like walking corpses. Caucasians also preferred greeting each other by shaking hands instead of the Hawaiian greeting of sharing breath known as honi. These elements made Hawaiians call Caucasians "haole," or "no breath," because haole combines "ha" for breath, and "'ole" for none.

Around Hawai'i's whaling age, Hawaiians left the islands for work or family, and the meaning of haole changed from "no breath" to "foreigner," or "someone not from Hawai'i," and kama'āina was used more frequently. Kama'āina means child of the land and was reserved for Hawaiians born in Hawai'i. Hawaiians born outside Hawai'i were called haole.

HAWAI'I'S NIGHTMARCHERS

NIGHTMARCHERS WERE THE GHOST procession of Hawai'i's ali'i and warriors. If your paths cross, they'll kill you and you'll join them.

Hawaiians called them huaka'i pō. Huaka'i means parade or procession. Pō means night. They announce themselves by beating drums or blowing conch shells. They are one of Hawai'i's most active supernatural beings and deadliest. Animals sense them before they are heard, and they've been encountered by people regardless of ethnicity, age, and education.

If you hear them, it's best to leave. If your ancestor is with them, they will protect you. If you don't have an ancestor among them, avoid looking at them. Not looking at an ali'i or their procession was practiced because seeing an ali'i was a way to steal their mana, or power, and the thief's immediate death restored the stolen mana. Thieves avoided death by making it to a place of refuge, or pu'uhonua, but they were difficult to reach.

Some believe you could avoid being killed by nightmarchers by removing your clothes or covering yourself in urine, but these theories are questionable.

Nightmarchers appear on Hawai'i's twenty-seventh moon phase known as pō Kāne or night of Kāne, the god—or "akua"—of nature, water, and life. These nights provided ali'i enough light to upkeep sacred places and heiaus, or temples. The ali'i also had the smallest shadow, since touching an ali'i's shadow was like touching them, which could make them lose mana.

Nightmarchers walk through obstacles in their path but avoid Hawaiian ti plants, or Cordyline fructosa. The plant's leaves, or ti leaves, are sacred to the Hawaiian god Lono and the goddess Laka and a main item used in ceremonies.

Many Hawaiian households plant ti leaves for luck but may divert nightmarchers to new paths.

A second nightmarcher procession of gods and demigods may exist. Not much is known about this rare procession, which might occur on pō Kāne, or the fourteenth night, pō Akua, which translates to night of the gods.

THE BOYS & THE TRAIL
Inspired by personal experience

As the moon waned over a Hawaiian night, a boy ran into the woods behind his house. Sweat stung his eyes as he reached the familiar mountain path. His pursuer erupted from bushes and tackled him.

It was the child's older cousin, who laughed and pinned the boy.

The child apologized and struggled, escaping.

A thud echoed up the path.

The boys silenced.

No cars roared from the highway. No insects chirped.

A thud broke the stillness.

Tears fell from the child's face. His cousin helped him up.

A conch shell trumpeted from the mountainside, and the children ran home.

THE IMAGINARY FRIEND
Inspired by folklore

A Hawaiian family lived in an old house raised on stilts, and like many locals, they used the crawl space for storage. Their son had an imaginary friend, but they didn't mind because it encouraged his creativity.

His parents rearranged their son's room, and the following morning, their son was sleeping on the floor instead of his bed.

They asked if he was okay.

He said he was and suggested his imaginary friend led him to the floor in the night.

His parents thought nothing of it but occasionally found him sleeping on the floor.

They shared their son's behavior with others. Someone recommended a kahuna, or someone knowledgeable in Hawai'i's mystic ways, to look at their house. They thought it was silly but contacted a kahuna.

The kahuna wandered through the house. In the child's room, the kahuna sensed a presence on the floor where the child would be found.

The kahuna theorized the parents had moved their child's bed into a nightmarcher's path and the presence led him out of their way before they passed.

The kahuna recommended placing ti plants around the house and checking the crawl space. Human remains were dug up in the crawl space beneath where they'd find their sleeping child.

KA'AHUMANU
HAWAI'I'S AMBITIOUS QUEEN

KA'AHUMANU WAS FROM THE island of Maui. Her ali'i father gave her to Kamehameha early in his campaign to unite the Hawaiian Islands.

She was much younger than Kamehameha but became his favorite wife and was a natural politician.

Ka'ahumanu didn't have any children, and Kamehameha's sacred wife, Keōpuolani, outranked her. When Kamehameha died, he was succeeded by his son with Keōpuolani, Liholiho.

Ka'ahumanu prevented losing her power by claiming the dying Kamehameha appointed her Kuhina Nui, which was similar to a prime minister and equal in power to Kamehameha.

She could not prove Kamehameha made this statement, but everyone accepted it. So Ka'ahumanu became Hawai'i's Kuhina Nui, equal to King Kamehameha II, Liholiho, and his mother, Keōpuolani, remained Hawai'i's queen consort.

More foreigners arrived in Hawai'i, and Ka'ahumanu noticed women ate with men. This violated the Hawaiian kapu, or law, but the gods didn't punish the foreigners.

Ka'ahumanu questioned Hawai'i's old ways and accepted Christianity. She befriended Liholiho's mother Keōpuolani, who also converted to Christianity.

They agreed to prove their new religion's power by inviting Liholiho to eat with them. The monarch was more interested in yachts, women, and alcohol but begrudgingly sat beside his mother and ate.

Hawaiians watched them eat unpunished by the gods, and a paradigm shift began. Liholiho abolished Hawai'i's kapu system, their old religion, and stopped the practice of hula, which missionaries considered too sexual.

Since the Hawaiian language was only verbal, the hula had served as a storehouse of Hawai'i's history, culture, and ways. When it stopped, Hawaiians lost a lot of their history, culture, and stories.

Heiaus, or temples, were burned with the figures of Hawai'i's gods. Ka'ahumanu, Keōpuolani, and missionaries provided Christianity as the kingdom's new religion, but Liholiho never converted.

About six years later, High Chiefess Kapi'olani, (not to be confused with Queen Kapi'olani, whom most Hawaiian places are named after) embraced Christianity. High Chiefess Kapi'olani went to Kilauea volcano with her Bible to prove Christianity was stronger than Hawai'i's goddess of fire Pele. High Chiefess Kapi'olani survived. Her demonstration convinced many Hawaiians to embrace Christianity and inspired the poet Alfred Lord Tennyson to write the poem, "Kapi'olani."

Since Kaua'i and Ni'ihau had voluntarily joined the Hawaiian Kingdom, rumors circulating about the acceptance of Christianity threatened to cause them to leave.

Kamehameha II, Liholiho, sailed his yacht to Kaua'i. He showed it off to the Kaua'i ali'i and sailed back to O'ahu with the ali'i. The ali'i was placed under house arrest and forced to marry Ka'ahumanu. When the ali'i died, Ka'ahumanu married one of the ali'i's sons to prevent a possible uprising.

Kamehameha II's mother Keōpuolani died, and Liholiho went to London. He and his court contracted measles, and the twenty-six-year-old king died in 1824. Their bodies were transported back to Hawai'i.

In 1825, the Hawaiian Kingdom went to Liholiho's eleven-year-old blood brother, Kamehameha III, Kauikeaouli, and Kaʻahumanu assisted the young monarch.

Kaʻahumanu was baptized, and her chosen name was Elizabeth, like Queen Elizabeth I.

Kaʻahumanu died in 1832. Her remains were placed in Nuʻuanu's Royal Mausoleum Mauna ʻAla, which means Fragrant Hills. The mausoleum contains all the Kamehamehas, except King Kamehameha the Great.

DUKE KAHANAMOKU

In 1890, Hawai'i is a kingdom, and Duke Paoa Kahinu Mokoe Hulikohola Kahanamoku was born in Kalia, an area of Waikiki. He was the oldest of five brothers and three sisters, whose family was descended from a low-ranked ali'i who served the higher class.

Duke attended Kamehameha Schools and McKinley High School, then became a Waikiki Beach boy to help his family.

The clean-cut Waikiki Beach boys were a historic symbol of Hawai'i. They were the island's first cultural guides, who were mainly Hawaiians who lived off tips from teaching tourists wealthy enough to visit the islands the Hawaiian customs of surfing, fishing, playing the ukulele, and canoe paddling.

Duke cultivated his aquatic, or waterman, abilities and surfed his sixteen-foot, one-hundred-and-fourteen-pound, skegless koa-wood surfboard papa nui, which means a big flat surface, or lumber.

In 1911, Duke broke three freestyle swimming world records at Honolulu Harbor and qualified for the US Olympic team. At the 1912 Stockholm Olympics, he won gold in the men's 100-meter freestyle and silver in the men's 4x200 freestyle relay.

Duke traveled with swimming exhibitions while teaching non-Polynesians how to surf and make surfboards, and Duke was known as the Big Kahuna.

World War I halted the 1916 Olympics. At the 1920 Antwerp Olympics, Duke defended his gold medal. He won, but a dispute caused a re-swim, and Duke won again with a new world record. Then Duke won his third gold medal in the men's 4x200-meter freestyle relay.

At the 1924 Paris Olympics, Duke, now thirty-three, matched his world record but took the silver. At the 1932 Los Angeles Olympics, he was an alternative on the US water polo team, which took the bronze. Many believe he would have won two more golds if the 1916 Olympics hadn't been canceled.

Duke briefly lived in LA and appeared in films and TV shows. He also rescued eight men with his surfboard at Newport Beach, a feat the Newport Beach police chief called "the most superhuman surfboard rescue act the world has ever seen."

Duke moved back to Hawai'i and was elected sheriff for the city and county of Honolulu. Duke married dance teacher Nadine Alexander, who had been enamored with him since she was a teenager. He was close friends with Doris Duke and received the title Hawai'i's Ambassador of Aloha.

In 1968, when Duke Kahanamoku was seventy-seven, he passed away from a heart attack. His ashes were scattered at Waikiki Beach while the song "Aloha 'Oe" played. "Aloha 'Oe" is a somber farewell song written by the Hawaiian Kingdom's Queen Lili'uokalani when she was a princess.

Duke Kahanamoku was born when Hawai'i was a kingdom and saw it become a territory. Then in 1959, it became a state.

He was the first person inducted into the Olympic Hall of Fame and the Swimming and Surfing Halls of Fame. He danced the hula with England's queen mother, Elizabeth, and his nine-foot-tall statue is near where his ashes were scattered.

Some Hawaiians criticized Duke's statue because his back faces the ocean. Hawaiians are taught to never turn your back on the ocean. But the statue was accepted and is one of Hawai'i's iconic landmarks.

GEORGE FREETH

George Freeth was a part-Hawaiian Waikiki Beach boy who helped popularize surfing in California. George had difficulty with his traditional surfboard and cut it in half, which many consider was the birth of the original longboard.

George was awarded a lifesaving medal for saving several fishermen with his longboard off Venice Beach and was credited with developing the rescue paddleboard.

THE ASWANG

THE PHILIPPINE SHAPESHIFTING VAMPIRE

A SWANGS LURK THROUGHOUT THE Philippines, but Panay's province of Capiz is the creature's home.

Aswang first appeared in folklore as the name of a god. But there does not seem to be a connection between the aswang god and the word's other meanings.

Aswang was an umbrella term for monsters or disturbances, and while the aswang creature is associated with the manananggal, many suggest they are different beings.

Aswangs are powerful during the day and almost unstoppable at night. Many believe the aswang got its name by combining the Tagalog words for salt (asin) and garlic (bawang), which are the creature's weakness. While most weapons wound the aswang, the effectiveness of holy water, religious locations, and certain weapons is questionable, and the creature's rapid healing makes it difficult to kill.

Aswangs can mimic voices and shape-shift into people, and large black animals like pigs, horses, and dogs. An aswang's human form is usually an attractive woman who sprouts claws and bat wings. These wings and a ticking sound tell you how close an aswang is. If the flapping wings and ticking is loud, an aswang is far. If the sounds are faint, an aswang is near.

This audible trickery allows them to close on its prey. Their ticking led some to call aswang, tik-tik.

Aswangs use their proboscis tongues to consume blood, organs, dead bodies, and children. Their favorite foods are unborn babies and human liver. After they feed, they may replace their victim with logs, tree palms, or a doppelgänger to avoid being detected. The victim's friends and loved ones may suspect the doppelgänger, but the clone will die after a few days.

Villagers perform rituals to protect the recently deceased. During wakes, sweeping is forbidden because it may spread the body's scent. When the body is moved, they release an injured chicken to distract nearby aswangs.

If an aswang joins a village, the creature hides its identity and kills outside the village. If villagers notice the aswang, they will leave it alone until village members go missing. Villagers have killed suspected aswangs within the past decade.

Anyone can become an aswang by staring at the moon on certain nights and keeping fertilized chicken eggs in their armpits or against their stomach because the chick is the source of an aswang's power. If the chick enters the person's body, they become an aswang. Aswangs can transfer their chick into someone by mouth. However, the new host will become an aswang, and the old host dies.

Aswangs are selfish and hunt alone even if they have a mate.

You can identify an aswang by looking into their eyes. If your reflection is upside down, the creature you are facing is an aswang. If you look between your legs at a subject and it's distorted, the subject is an aswang. Some believe aswangs' feet are backward. If this is true, it could mean their shape-shifting is flawed.

ASWANGS IN PHILIPPINE HISTORY

The Spanish, needing labor for their settlements, used aswangs to scare Filipinos from the jungle into the city to be converted to Catholicism. Settlers also killed villagers but blamed it on aswangs, and vilified female freedom fighter leaders by claiming they were aswangs. This may explain why aswangs are usually female.

During World War II, Filipinos spread rumors about aswangs living in the forest, which prevented Japanese from invading.

ASWANGS IN FILIPINO CULTURE

Filipinos call their unpopular politicians aswangs. The popular urban myth "Maria Labo" is about an aswang-like creature, and there was an aswang festival until the church stopped it.

GENETIC MUTATION

The genetic disorder X-linked dystonia-parkinsonism or XDP or Lubag Syndrome is associated with the aswang. The mutation started generations ago and remains dormant until the carrier reaches their thirties or forties.

Once active, the disorder causes severe muscle spasms, muscle cramps, and prevents the carrier from walking and talking.

These individuals live in the jungle because they are poor and only have their community. But once they exhibit symptoms, the individual eventually loses body control—and their community because they believe the carrier is an aswang.

Carriers commit suicide, die from malnutrition, or are killed by their village.

Symptoms appear late in the carrier's life after they've passed the dormant mutation to their children.

As of this writing, there is no cure.

THE JEALOUS GOD
Inspired by folklore

When people didn't know how to make fire, a god supplied it. They loved the god, but a jealous god called Aswang desired the people's love.

Aswang asked the god for some of the sacred fire.

The god refused, knowing Aswang couldn't handle it.

But Aswang stole the sacred flame and fled. As he ran, the flame became an inferno that spread across the land. The fires created monsters and endangered the people.

The god confronted Aswang, reclaimed the sacred flame, and stopped the fires. Aswang was despised by the people and cursed by the god.

THE WAKE'S VISITATION
Inspired by folklore

The night's shadows created an unsettling mood in an old man's wake. As the attendees wiped their grief-worn eyes, the jungle's noisy insects outside their walls fell silent.

Wide-eyed women gripped their children.

Men clustered outside the entrance. One shined his flashlight into the dense foliage.

A dozen yards away, the darkness devoured his beam.

A shadow beside a tree moved.

The men stepped back.

The shade's white fangs pierced the dark. It revealed itself as a snarling large black dog.

The men glanced at their loved ones and their departed's body. A man stepped toward the beast.

It lunged at him.

The men screamed, and the man jumped back into their arms.

The elderly widow parted them.

They urged her back.

She swatted their hands, wiped tears from her tired eyes, and shuffled toward the dog.

The dog tilted its head.

The shuffling widow tried shooing it away.

The beast growled and flashed its white fangs.

The widow yelled, pointing at the jungle.

The dog barked with snapping jaws.

The widow screamed and threw salt at it.

The dog's mouthful of salt turned its bark into a whine. It fell back upon itself and retreated to the forest.

Tears streamed from the widow as she yelled.

The jungle's insects resumed their song.

She shuffled to the men, batted their hands away, and returned to the wake.

THE EXPECTING MOTHER
Inspired by folklore

A mother helped her pregnant daughter into bed. "Well, Olivia. Maybe tomorrow you won't run off like you did this morning."

Olivia sighed. She had spent all day explaining herself, but it didn't matter. Mother enjoyed hearing herself talk, and her nagging wouldn't become irritating until dinner. But Olivia needed a break before eating her omelet. Being whale-sized didn't help.

"Your baby's due any day now. You shouldn't draw attention to yourself."

Olivia refrained from telling her mother how annoying she was. Mother always meant well. Perspiration formed on Olivia's forehead. Her husband, Manuel, should be home soon, and she hoped he'd shower before coming to bed.

Mother closed the window.

Olivia sat up. "What are you doing? It's hot."

Mother smirked. "But the aswang."

Olivia grimaced. *We almost made it a day without her mentioning that stupid creature.* Last night's nightmare of the horrid monster eating her baby haunted her. Sharing them always made them less scary, but Mother's nagging would worsen. *Manuel needs to be home.* Olivia's stomach wretched. She forced her food down and rubbed her belly.

Olivia's baby moved, and the expectant mother's muscles relaxed.

Mother kissed her head. "Good night."

"Good night."

Mother went to her room, and her door closed.

Finally. Olivia closed her eyes. The pillow was hot. She adjusted, and the sheets tangled around her house-sized body. She whipped everything off, struggled from bed, waddled to the window, and opened it. The night was still, but a gentle breeze against her damp skin was heavenly. The wind died, and she returned to bed. Flapping wings faintly drifted on another breeze. Damn bats. A low snore rumbled from Olivia as she drifted to sleep.

On the rooftop over her bed, an aswang retracted its wings. It became a naked woman, and its eyes glistened in the moonlight. Her nostrils flared, sniffing the air. The creature's long hair draped the roof as it placed her ear against it.

Down the hall, an old woman snored. Below the creature, the pregnant one's breathing slowed as she slipped deeper into sleep. Her unborn child's heartbeat pricked the aswang's ears.

The creature licked its lips and crept to the roof's edge. Its tongue went over the side and slipped into the window. The room's scent allowed the aswang to see its layout, and her tongue went toward the bed.

Olivia played with her toddler in a field. The toddler fell. Its face twisted, and it cried. Olivia ran to her child but couldn't reach the screaming baby.

Olivia woke and sat up in bed.

A figure in her room filled the window.

She screamed.

"Olivia, it's okay. It's me," Manuel said.

"Manuel? What are you doing by the window?"

"I just got home and closed it."

Mother burst in, and the lights erupted.

Olivia and Manuel shielded their eyes and complained.

Mother scanned the room. "What's wrong?"

"We're fine, Mother. I just had a bad dream."

Mother studied them, then turned off the lights. She sniffed the air, her eyes rolled toward the ceiling, and she left.

Manuel joined his wife in bed.

She hit him for scaring her and turned away.

Manuel spooned her. His hot breath graced her neck. His breathing stopped. He moved from her and rubbed the area between them.

"What's wrong?" Oliva said.

"The bed's wet. Were you that scared?"

She felt for her child.

It didn't move.

Her heart raced, her breathing shallowed, and a tear slipped from her eye.

Manuel jumped from bed and tossed the sheets. He gasped. "It's your water. Your water broke. We need to get you to the hospital."

Olivia's child kicked, and the hungry aswang flew away.

THE ASWANG & THE CHILD
Inspired by folklore

The village roosters crowed as the aswang glowered at the rising sun and returned to her hut. Her tongue prodded her mouth wounds from the salt another village's old woman had thrown at her. The creature's growling stomach reminded her of last night's unsuccessful hunt. She cursed and hit her table. Its vials of potions rattled, and she sulked in the shadows.

The villagers beyond her walls began their day. At their scent, her stomach panged. They only bothered her for medicine, and if they turned on her, she'd flee to the jungle where she'd be vulnerable.

The memory of human meat danced on her tongue, especially that of children. Drool dripped on her hands. The village children's scent always triggered the memory of a child she had eaten years ago. The aswang lost herself to the nostalgic imprint.

Someone cleared their throat.

The aswang backed against the shadowed wall.

A wide-eyed little girl stood at her door.

The aswang giggled, emerged from the shadows, and beckoned her.

The child entered.

Laughter burst from the aswang. She covered her grinning mouth.

The girl approached.

The aswang's claw touched the child's hair. The creature's skin prickled.

The girl smirked at her upside-down reflection in the aswang's bloodshot eyes.

The creature's claw glided to the girl's cheek. *It'd be so easy. I could devour you before the rooster crows.* The creature snatched its claw and darted into the shadows. Its shaking claw pointed to a bottle on her cluttered table.

The girl picked up a familiar container and went to the door. She stopped in its frame.

The aswang's breathing sharpened. *What are you doing, child?*

The girl grabbed something outside the hut.

The aswang crouched. *The child has what she wants, and now she'll kill me. But I'll strike first.* A low growl filled the air.

The girl held a sack. Something in it moved and clucked. She tossed the sack before the aswang.

It leaped for it.

Feathers exploded from the sack and drifted throughout the room.

The aswang chomped on the chicken while focused on the girl's scent.

The teary-eyed girl ran home with the medicine as a rooster crowed.

THE MĀORI PATUPAIAREHE

PATUPAIAREHE ARE ALSO KNOWN as turehu, or pakepakeha. They have magical abilities and are not fairies but wood spirits who will torment those who disrespect the woods.

Patupaiarehe hate the sun. They appear at night as short humans with blue or green eyes, red hair, and fair skin. They eat raw meat, are repulsed by cooked food, and scared by fire.

The patupaiarehe lures attractive women by playing bone flutes. Māoris with patupaiarehe traits are called Urukehu and were believed to be the product of a woman lured by a patupaiarehe.

Patupaiarehe know many things, and the Māoris gained some of their knowledge.

THE CLEVER CHIEF
Inspired by folklore

Chief Kahukura traveled north but underestimated the approaching night and slept on sand dunes beside an empty beach.

Voices and laughter woke him.

Kahukura discovered patupaiarehe net fishing on the nearby beach. He knew of patupaiarehe, but Māoris didn't know about nets.

The chief wanted the nets. If he could stall the patupaiarehe until dawn, they'd flee from the sun, abandoning their nets.

Kahukura, barely taller than a patupaiarehe, joined them.

As the patupaiarehe fished, Kahukura sabotaged their nets until the sun rose.

The patupaiarehe abandoned their nets, and Kahukura shared them with his people.

KIDNAPPED
Inspired by folklore

As the village prepared for an uncomfortable New Zealand night, a young man wished his grandmother good night and went to bed. He woke while being carried into the woods with people talking and laughing around him. He tried to move but couldn't.

He sat up in bed. It was morning.

His grandmother asked if he was all right.

He shared his dream with her.

She frowned. "You're lucky they returned you."

THE BEAUTIFUL PATUPAIAREHE
Inspired by folklore

A patupaiarehe loved eating shellfish while watching the night mist on Waitematā Harbour.

She tossed her red hair and picked another morsel.

A man greeted her.

She screamed and fled to a nearby dune. Her stomach growled, and she looked back at her meal.

The man offered her the shellfish and collected a few more for her.

She was taken by him, and they continued meeting under the stars. Love blossomed, but she realized a relationship couldn't work between a mortal and patupaiarehe. She told him they needed to stop seeing each other.

But their love was too strong, and they tried to make things work. She met his family, who accepted her and built her a hut that blocked the sun. The couple married and had several beautiful children while the happy patupaiarehe did what was needed of her at night.

She was an expert weaver, and the craft was unknown to Māoris.

Women asked her to teach them. She agreed and taught them outside to accommodate everyone. But she lost track of time, and the rising sun scared her back to her realm where the heartbroken patupaiarehe remained, longing for her husband and children.

This is how Māoris learned how to weave.

WASHINGTON STATE'S WALKER-AMES HOUSE

T HE WALKER-AMES HOUSE IS a Queen Anne–style Victorian house on Washington state's Kitsap Peninsula.

The Peninsula was named after Suquamish Native American chief Kitsap, and the area is known as Teekalet, or "brightness of the noonday sun."

Nearby, Port Gamble was established for the lumber trade and named after Lieutenant Colonel John M. Gamble or Lieutenant Robert Gamble.

The lumber mill superintendent occupied the house, but records are unclear whether Walker was his first or last name. Walker retired and passed the house to his son-in-law, Edwin Ames, and the house was known as the Walker-Ames house.

The house has hidden spaces and false walls. Unusual activity began being reported in the fifties. Activity included lights turning on or off, a nanny or child appearing in the upstairs window every six weeks, cold spots, and apparitions. Children are heard playing or running on the second floor. The basement contains foul smells, and something hits women and pulls their hair or jackets.

The lumber mill's closure and unknown history of what haunts the house caused people to believe the town fabricated these stories for tourism.

The house's last resident moved out in 1995.

THE NEWLYWED'S HONEYMOON
Inspired by folklore

A newlywed couple put their money toward a home and spent a budget-friendly honeymoon in Port Gamble. The wife longed for children and took every opportunity to greet everyone she passed. She loved how they zoomed past on their bikes and waved from upstairs windows and porches. While gushing about them at a general store, she mentioned the house beside the store had a peculiar child in the upstairs window.

The store owner chuckled. "Miss, no one's lived there for years."

THE TEENAGERS & THE HOUSE
Inspired by folklore

Hours after the last moving truck emptied the Walker-Ames house, the night wind carried the loud whispers of six teenagers approaching the house. The equal group of boys and girls grew up seeing the house and hearing its stories, and tonight they were going to explore it. Fueled with nervous excitement from the latest *X-Files* episode, they went around the back and discovered an unlocked door.

"The movers must've forgotten to lock it," a guy said.

"Are you sure about this?" a girl asked.

"Yeah. If anyone sees us, they'll think we're the movers." He ignited his flashlight. "Let's go."

The teens lit their flashlights. Several hid their chattering teeth as the group clustered and entered. The teens inched into the hallway, and their frantic flashlight beams and wide eyes darted throughout the shadow-filled room.

"Hey," a teenage guy said. "We should pair up to better… explore the house."

His girlfriend giggled and grabbed his side.

The others hesitantly paired up and ventured deeper into the dark house.

A couple descended the creaking basement stairs. Fear heightened their intoxicating hormones until, at the foot of the stairs, they turned off their flashlights and kissed. Burning passion overwhelmed them, and their breathing deepened.

Pain interrupted the girl. "Hey, ease up on my hair."

Her date's eyes contracted. "I'm not pulling your hair."

A shadow moved behind him.

She screamed.

He spun around and ignited his light.

A humanoid shadow scurried into the far wall.

The couple yelled and scrambled upstairs.

Dark figures filled the door.

The girl screamed.

"What's going on?" the figures said. "We heard screaming."

The figures were their friends. The girl fell into one of their arms.

Her date explained what happened.

Running sounds on the second floor raced above them.

The girl comforting her friend looked at the ceiling. "I didn't know they went upstairs."

Her date smirked. "They better get down here fast; we're leaving."

The last couple emerged from a hallway room.

The boyfriend adjusted his pants. "Who went upstairs?"

The wide-eyed group stepped back from the couple.

The couple noticed their friends were looking past them and turned around.

A dark figure loomed in a door.

The screaming teens fled, and the porch light turned on.

VANUATU'S MYSTERY ISLAND

M YSTERY ISLAND'S ORIGINAL NAME was Inyeug, which means small island. Inyeug is one of the forty islands and islets of Vanuatu, settled by Melanesians around 1300 BCE. They left Mystery Island alone because they believed evil spirits, or their ancestor's ghosts, dwelled there. If they visited the island, they'd leave before nightfall.

Millennia later, in 1606 CE, Portuguese explorer Pedro Fernandes de Queirós landed in Vanuatu and named the Big Island Espiritu Santo. Later explorers included Louis Antoine de Bougainville and Captain Cook.

There are two theories as to why Inyeug was nicknamed Mystery Island. The first occurred in the seventies or eighties during Queen Elizabeth II's visit. Journalist were confused about Inyeug meaning small island, and they reported it as Mystery Island.

The second theory involves public relations person Ron Connelly. When asked about Inyeug, he stated he's never been to the island because there's nowhere to anchor. So the island was a mystery to him.

Mystery Island is now a port of call for cruise lines where weddings are held, and Melanesians share their culture, arts, and crafts with tourists.

ENSLAVING PACIFIC ISLANDERS

Blackbirding is the practice of enslaving native Pacific Islanders, who were called blackbirds. This began around 1860, when European settlements and plantations needed manual labor. The blackbirding crews frequented Mystery Island because it was uninhabited.

As of this writing, blackbirding still occurs.

CULTURAL SLUR

An abbreviated Hawaiian word for male laborer is kanaka. Kanaka is also an accepted Hawaiian pidgin word for a male Hawaiian or Pacific Islander, but some South Pacific cultures consider kanaka a racial slur.

THE SERPENT & THE REEF
Inspired by folklore

In the beginning, there was the Pacific Ocean. A massive sea serpent broke the horizon.

The serpent became tired and roared, "Let the reef rise!"

The reef rose, and the creature rested on the dry land before continuing its journey.

This is how Vanuatu's many islands and islets were created.

THE CANNIBAL GHOST
Inspired by folklore

A group of brothers climbed a tree to collect material for armbands. The youngest rushed his climbing to catch up to his brothers but fell and died. His ghost smelled the brothers in the tree.

The brothers confirmed they heard the fall.

The oldest craned his neck to look around the branches below. "What fell?"

The youngest brother's ghost licked its lips and climbed the tree. "I stepped on a branch. It broke and fell."

The brothers collected their materials, agreed to return to their village, and started climbing down.

Their brother's ghost saw them, scurried from the tree, covered its body with leaves, and greeted his brothers as they reached the ground.

The brothers studied the ghost. "Are you okay? You don't look good."

"I'm fine," the ghost said. "I'm just tired."

"Yes, it's been a long day." The brothers followed the path to their village.

Their brother's ghost couldn't abandon his body but needed the brothers to guide it to the village. After several yards, it stopped. "I forgot something at the tree. Don't leave until I'm back." It retrieved its body and hid it before rejoining the brothers.

They resumed their walk, and the ghost stopped them several times. At the outskirts of their village, the first night's stars twinkled, and the brothers followed the ghost. They discovered their youngest brother had died and his ghost was fooling them.

They ran to their village and warned everyone to shut their doors because something mysterious was coming. Everyone obeyed, but a grandmother and her grandson didn't hear the warning.

The ghost entered the village and threw its body into a house's doorframe, but it struck the closed door. The ghost collected its corpse and did this to every house.

At the grandmother's house, the body sailed through the door and landed inside. The grandmother threw the body out, but the ghost caught it and threw it back.

This continued until the tired grandmother accidentally threw her grandson instead of the body.

The ghost laughed. "I'll enjoy eating this child."

"Wait," the grandmother said. "Will the sun harm you?"

The ghost's eyes narrowed. "It will."

The grandmother laughed. "You better hurry to wherever you came from. The sun rises soon."

The ghost cringed. "No, it won't. I saw the first night's stars a little while ago."

The grandson cried.

His grandmother contained her fear and argued with the ghost.

The sun rose. The ghost became taro and his body became bark.

The crying grandson ran into his grandmother. She comforted him and smiled at the new day.

AMAROK
THE GREAT WOLF SPIRIT

T HE AMAROK IS A wolf spirit from Inuit mythology. Some suggest Amarok is not the same as the trickster wolf god Amaguq, or the creature known as Shunka Warak'in, and conflicting records are unclear if the Amarok and waheela are the same creature.

The Amarok is a mystic creature that resembles a giant white wolf, or dire wolf. The Amarok was created to eat sick or weak caribou while healthy caribou were enjoyed by humans. However, Amarok will attack hunters at night.

Witnesses have claimed seeing an Amarok-like creature. Zoologist have stated if these reports are true, it may signal the return of a dire wolf, or another prehistoric wolf.

THE AMAROK & THE BOY
Inspired by folklore

A frail boy called to the spirit of strength and wished to be stronger. An Amarok appeared and agreed to help. The creature's tail hit the boy. Small bones fell from the child's body.

"These bones were hindering you," the Amarok said.

The Amarok trained the boy and continued hitting the bad bones out of him. The boy grew into a man who defeated three bears and became his village's champion.

THE HUNTER
Inspired by folklore

The arctic moon slipped behind clouds as a hunter entered the cave beside the lake. Whimpering animals stirred his curiosity, and near the back of the cave, he found the Amarok's pups.

The hunter smiled at his prize, killed them, and began to leave.

He stopped near the entrance and admired the view.

The Amarok broke from the forest.

The hunter retreated into the cave, hid beside his kills, and readied to engage their mother.

At the cave's entrance, the Amarok stopped and sniffed the air. It dashed to the lake and clamped onto something in the water. The snarling Amarok pulled a humanoid shadow from the lake as the hunter's body collapsed.

The Amarok had pulled the hunter's soul from his body, for nothing remains hidden from the Amarok.

THE NIGHT HUNT
Inspired by folklore

His sick wife's image was engraved on his eyelids, and their child's coughing echoed in his head. Lugging his kill, he ignored the protest of his burning legs, hoping to get home before the impending blizzard.

Hours earlier, his wife had wanted to reward him with a meal. But she underestimated her sickness, and she accidentally ruined their food.

He wasn't mad and embraced her as she apologized.

He cleaned the area and studied the night. He was a hunter like his ancestors, and while the Amarok made night hunting deadly, his family needed food.

Now, weighted down with his kill, he struggled through the blaring, moonlit snow that sapped his remaining energy and encouraged his eyes to close.

He saw the reflected eyes of animals lurking in the surrounding woods.

The blizzard's keeping them away. The approaching storm must be massive.

His legs buckled, and he fell.

Fatigue made him curse and yell.

A paw print in the snow silenced him.

It was twice the size of his hand. He assumed it was a bear, but it was a wolf. He stood while scanning the tracks. They went behind him to a distant rise where a sitting wolf watched him.

Fear made his stomach drop. Amarok.

The Amarok's white fur glowed in the moonlight. Its eyes were black holes, and though it looked normal-sized, the distance implied the animal was bigger than a bear.

It stood, stepped toward him, and stopped at the rise's edge.

The hunter stepped back.

The Amarok growled. Its curling lip revealed sharp fangs.

The hunter checked the woods beside him. The stalking animals were gone. He faced the Amarok. It was gone.

The Amarok's growl whispered in his ear.

Grabbing his kill, he stumbled in the snow toward home.

Snowflakes whipped in his eyes, and the Amarok's silhouette blurred among the trees beside him. It raced ahead, seeming to fly over the snowdrifts.

The hunter went from stepping over the snow to plowing through it. His cabin was in the clearing.

Branches snapped overhead. A curtain of snow poured from the trees and shoved him. He scrambled from the growing frozen entombment.

The Amarok's howl pierced his soul with dread.

He dashed for his shelter as the howl blended with the blizzard's roar.

The blizzard's onslaught slammed his door against the wall as he entered. He freed himself from his kill and struggled to close the door.

Inches from the frame, snarling joined the blizzard's roar.

The exhausted hunter lost ground.

His wife took his side, and they battled against the blizzard and snarling fighting to enter.

The couple's muscles burned as they moved the door. It shut, and his wife bolted it. He embraced her and went to see their crying child.

He told his wife about his hunt. She was Inuit but didn't believe in the ways of their past and suggested he had experienced snow blindness.

He agreed but never told her about the large wolf tracks that circled their cabin the following morning.

NAFANUA
SAMOA'S GODDESS OF WAR

NAFANUA WAS CREATED BY a blood clot from her parents. Her father was Saveasi'uleo, who some refer to as Elo. Elo was the god of the Samoan underworld, Pulotu. Her mother was Tilafaiga, one of the conjoined twins who brought the art of tatau, or tattooing, to Samoa.

Nafanua's items were made from toa, or koa wood. The letters *T* and *K* are replaced in some Polynesian cultures. This was how Captain Cook conversed with Hawaiians, thanks to his previous South Pacific expeditions.

The entrance to the underworld, Pulotu, was in Falealupo, the west end of Savai'i Island. Falealupo was where Nafanua's relatives lived and where she governed. Many traveled to Falealupo seeking Nafanua's advice in war and governance. It's unclear how or when she died, but toward the end of her reign, a king asked her to help him unite Samoa.

Nafanua replied, "Wait on the heavens for a crown for your kingdom."

In 1830, missionaries arrived. The king's son, Malietoa Vainu'upo, joined them and united Samoa.

Nafanua's rule established the chiefly government of fa'amatai, which is active as of this writing.

Nafanua's name became a unisex title and remains one of Samoa's highest legendary titles. In 1988, the Nafanua title was bestowed on Dr. Paul Alan Cox for his work in saving Samoa's rainforests.

THE GREAT BATTLE
Inspired by folklore

In Samoa's past, when women were considered inferior to men, the island Savai'i was ravaged by warring villages of the east and west until eastern Samoan ali'i Lilomaiava conquered the west.

Lilomaiava humiliated the western villagers by making them painfully climb a coconut tree feet-first. But he didn't know one of his victims was Ta'ii, the brother of the god of the underworld Saveasi'uleo.

Saveasi'uleo was enraged and sent his daughter Nafanua to free their western people.

Nafanua woke on a beach of Savai'i. A western village couple helped her, and Nafanua considered them her adoptive parents.

Nafanua's father Elo instructed her to cut down a toa tree and craft four items. Ta Fesilafa'i was a giant hook with sharp teeth on its shank opposite its gap. Fa'auli'ulito was a heavy, rounded stick similar to a billy club. Ulimasao was a canoe paddle with a pointed edge like a spade, meant to signal the war's end. The last item was the weapon of death, Fa'amategataua. It was a spear with sharp teeth where the blade met the staff. This was Nafanua's deadliest weapon, which could kill mortals and her divine family.

Nafanua's father Elo warned her to stop fighting when she reached their family's village.

Nafanua agreed. She enchanted her items with power from Pulotu and armed herself with her first weapon, Ta Fesilafa'i.

Nafanua asked her adoptive parents if they'd fight to stop Lilomaiava's forces. Her adoptive parents confessed they didn't know how to fight. Nafanua gave them her second item, Fa'auli'ulito, the billy club, but warned them to stay at the edge of the battlefield because she may not recognize them in her rage.

Lilomaiava's warriors didn't stand a chance against Nafanua as the goddess plowed through them with her battle hook. Waves of warriors attacked, but they were severely outmatched.

Along the perimeter, her adoptive parents' vengeance grew as they enjoyed beating the warriors. The couple wandered onto the battlefield and were accidentally killed by Nafanua in her blood rage. The goddess continued her merciless onslaught and reached her family's village.

Nafanua forgot her father's warning as droves of warriors converged on her. The goddess wiped her brow, readied herself, and a gust of wind blew against her damp skin. The coolness felt good, but Nafanua realized the wind had lifted her coverings and revealed her breasts.

The warriors halted. Humiliated to be bested by a woman, they surrendered, and Nafanua became Samoa's ultimate ali'i.

ORANG MINYAK
MALAYSIA'S OILY MAN

ORANG MINYAK, OR OILY man, has been considered a ghost, a shaman, or someone trying to obtain supernatural powers. It's unknown when he first appeared, but he was popularized after several films.

He can shape-shift into a dog or swarm of mosquitos but commonly appears as a naked man covered in black oil, which is how he got his name.

The oil doesn't leave his skin. It makes him difficult to grab and allows him to blend into the night. He rarely uses weapons and flees once discovered.

He steals luxury items and targets women for sex, particularly virgins, which may be part of a pact to ensure his supernatural abilities. He sneaks into women's bedrooms and uses mind control to prevent them from resisting him.

Women avoid him by not going out at night. They keep their male relatives' sweaty clothes in their bedroom or disguise themselves by wearing men's clothing.

Orang Minyak hates banana hearts and taro leaves, so people put these around their house. To kill an Orang Minyak, you have to bite off his big toe and cover him with Indonesian batik cloth.

Local women and tourists reported encountering him. He was seen within the past ten years as of this writing.

THE INTRUDER
Inspired by folklore

A college student danced beneath a streetlight on her way home from a date. She relived mispronouncing her order and enjoying red wine instead of white. She couldn't believe how beautiful her date, Sophie, was and how kissing her felt right.

Her childhood friends always talked about boys. She ignored feeling something was wrong with her and hoped some guy would catch her eye.

But now everything felt right.

She didn't know what to wear but remembered Sophie loved the only dress she owned.

She twirled under another streetlight until the hem reached her knees.

I'll have to thank Mother for this dress. She'd be thrilled seeing me in it instead of boy's clothes. Oh god, Mother. What would she and Dad think? There were lesbians back home in Indonesia. Did her parents know any? What would they think about Sophie?

Questions flooded her mind as she entered her flat. She tossed her purse on the nightstand and flopped onto her couch. Remembering beautiful Sophie calmed her. But the shadows in her apartment seemed to drain the color from the walls and her pictures. Even the colorful family blanket beside her was muted.

Her door opened.

She raised an eyebrow. *That's odd. But it's natural for doors to open.*

A shadow entered. Its eyes glowed red.

It's only natural for things to enter an open door. I must be dreaming.

The approaching shadow became a naked, muscular man.

She laughed. *There's no way a guy would walk around naked and enter my flat. This has to be a dream.*

He smiled and mounted her.

Of course, I discover I'm a lesbian and dream of this. My subconscious must be testing me.

His hand slipped under her dress.

Okay, I'm done with— Wait, I can't move. Oh God, this is real.

His nails slid along her skin.

Beeping erupted from her purse as her phone received a text message.

The startled man scurried from her.

Clarity surfaced in her foggy mind and brought the childhood story of Orang Minyak.

She grabbed the family blanket beside her and kneed him.

He fell off.

She followed him, spreading her blanket between them.

He tried escaping, but she pinned him while tucking the blanket under him. She crawled toward his feet, which were protruding from the blanket, grabbed his foot, and bit his big toe.

Her teeth clicked together. It felt like she bit air.

He roared below her and dissipated into the floor.

She caught her breath as color in her apartment regained its vibrancy. She checked under her blanket.

He was gone.

She wiped sweat from her brow. *I need a drink.*

Her text message was from Sophie, who thanked her for their date and asked if she wanted to get a drink.

Girl, you read my mind.

She grabbed her purse, headed for the door, and glanced at her blanket on the ground.

If college doesn't work out, I could be a paranormal exterminator.

MAE NAK
BANGKOK'S GHOST WIFE

MAE NAK IS ALSO known as Mae Nak Phra Khanong, which translates to Mother Nak of Phra Khanong.

She is connected with a woman from 1899 named Amdaeng Nak, who had a son and died while pregnant with her second child. Many believe pregnant women who die during childbirth are susceptible to becoming a disruptive ghost.

Amdaeng Nak's son did not want his father to remarry. He fabricated his mother's ghost story, dressed as a ghost, and threw rocks at people.

Those who don't accept this explanation believe her ghost is contained in a waistband owned by the royal family.

A shrine to Mae Nak at Wat Mahabut temple is a popular attraction. Originally, people offered dresses, pictures, and toys for her unborn child with the hope their loved one's may not to be drafted into Thailand's military. Now visitors request this or lucky lottery numbers while expectant mothers keep their distance from the shrine.

THE DEVOTED WIFE
Inspired by folklore

Around 1899, in Thailand's Phra Khanong District, Mae Nak experienced complications with her pregnancy. She wished to see her conscripted husband return safely from war and show him their new baby. But the labor was too much, and she passed with her unborn child.

Her husband, unaware of what happened, returned home. Mae Nak welcomed him with their healthy baby.

Mae Nak's husband adjusted to home life, but friends and neighbors acted unusual. Some planned to meet in private to tell him something but went missing or died.

He joined his wife as she prepared lunch. "What do you think about the strange events our friends are encountering?"

"Forget about that. Our family is all that matters."

He agreed, but something wasn't right.

Mae Nak dropped a lime.

He went to retrieve it, but Mae Nak's arm stretched to the ground and got it.

Her husband's eyes bulged. My wife is a ghost. *That's what everyone was trying to tell me, and she silenced them.* He hid his grief over losing his family and friends. When night fell, he fled to the nearby temple, Wat Mahabut.

Mae Nak discovered he was gone and pursued him.

He evaded her and reached Wat Mahabut.

Wat Mahabut's hallowed ground stopped Mae Nak. She screamed for her husband along its perimeter, then unleashed her fury on the district.

As the citizens scrambled among the devastation, an exorcist knew he could stop the entity and confronted Mae Nak.

She belted a blood-curdling yell and attacked him.

The exorcist stood his ground and entrapped her in a bottle. He prayed Mae Nak would find peace and threw the bottle in a nearby canal, hoping the bottle would be taken out to sea and the vengeful spirit would weaken.

Years later, fishermen found Mae Nak's bottle and freed her.

She continued her destructive path, searching for her husband and the exorcist who captured her.

A venerable monk familiar with Mae Nak's story confronted her and offered her peace.

But she attacked him.

He chanted a mantra. His eyes glowed, and he imprisoned her in his waistband.

The citizens demanded the ghost be destroyed.

The monk assured them that her spirit needed sympathy, but they refused to hear it.

The monk protected Mae Nak's ghost from the riot and knew the temple wouldn't be enough to protect her. He went to the palace and pleaded his trouble to the king.

The king understood his people, the monk, and pitied Mae Nak's spirit. He accepted the waistband and promised to keep it safe.

The royal family still has the waistband containing Mae Nak's ghost.

EL CUERO
CHILE'S AQUATIC TIGER MONSTER

E L Cuero translates to leather or hide, which witnesses claim describes the creature's skin.

El Cuero was first documented in Father Juan Ignacio Molina's 1810 essay on Chile's natural history. El Cuero is a stingray with a barbless tail. Its fringe is sharp like claws, and its eyes are on stocks like a snail. It can get up to five feet wide and weight around sixty-five pounds.

It attacks by wrapping around its prey, digging its sharp fringe into its victim's skin, and then its proboscis-like tongue sucks its prey's blood and/or organs.

El Cuero's ferociousness gave it the nickname the aquatic tiger and may be the same creature others know as Hueke-Hueke.

El Cuero can be killed by tossing sharp cactus into the water beside it. The creature will wrap around the cactus and stab itself to death.

Locals blame the El Cuero for unexplained drownings, and scientists believe it may be a predatory stingray.

THE RIVER BY THE VILLAGE
Inspired by folklore

Animals scattered as the children's game expanded from their South American village into the rainforest.

A nearby river silenced the sweaty children.

They gathered along the tree line, mesmerized by the shimmering water that their parents forbade them from entering.

A boy leaped toward the stream.

His friends yelled for him to come back.

He called his friends to join him swimming.

Several imagined being scolded by their parents and cried.

The boy darted for the river. He stopped at the bank.

A silence loomed.

A bunch of leaves floating in the middle of the water didn't drift downriver.

Yelling erupted behind the children, and a parent scolded them as she rounded them up and hurried them back to the village.

Wind rustled the trees as the floating leaves sank and swam away.

THE HONEYMOON HIKE
Inspired by folklore

He wanted to surprise his wife with her favorite junk food. But his plans backfired, and he faced spending their honeymoon's first day cleaning the cakey, sticky mess from their tent.

Lugging the tent to the river was a chore. He hoped to run into their guide for some help, but the guide must have gone somewhere else.

He approached the river to wash the cake out. The water sent a chill up his leg. As he emptied water from the tent. The material pressed against him.

This river has a strong current. He pushed back and encountered resistance. *Wait, this river wouldn't have such a current.*

A dense wall was behind the tent.

The wall rose.

His knees hit the underwater rocks.

The tent engulfed him, and he fell back into the water.

An air pocket formed around him. He regained his footing and tried standing.

The wall beyond the canvas thrashed, something circular pressed into the canvas shielding his hand.

He stood.

The wall slid off and splashed away.

He tossed the tent.

Yelling came from the riverbank.

His guide was wide-eyed on the shore with a machete. His wife, beside their guide, peeked over her hands.

"Get out of the water," they yelled.

He hurried to them, and his wife embraced him.

Their guide examined him. "He looks fine."

The husband raised an eyebrow. "Why wouldn't I be?"

His wife sobbed and explained a giant stingray attacked him. Their guide cut a thorny plant, threw it beside the creature, and it swam away.

"You are very lucky, sir." Their guide nodded at the jungle. "I feel it is best we return to camp for our belongings, go back to town, and you may decide if you wish to continue."

They left and the El Cuero drifted downriver.

GHOST MONTH

G HOST MONTH IS THE seventh lunar month. It's considered the most dangerous time of year because ghosts and spirits from the lower realms, or hell, wander the earth.

Ghost month's origins are unknown and might have started pre-Buddha. Many Asian cultures believe the number seven is unlucky, which could relate to the seventh lunar month being the worst.

Families burn fake money, or ghost money, and paper representing luxurious items as offerings to their departed ancestors.

Businesses provide offerings to ghosts in return for the spirits' blessings. Theaters reserve their first two rows for ghosts while venues perform old operas.

Nonbelievers respect this as a period of ancestor worship and remembrance.

Spirits are strongest at night, so it is bad luck to stay out late. Other ways to avoid bad luck include not going on vacation, avoiding life-changing events like getting married, starting a relationship, new job, or investing in new endeavors. Avoiding swimming is important because water is a strong conductor for ghosts who may drown swimmers.

THE YOUNG WOMAN AT THE LAKE
Inspire by folklore

The crescent moon hid behind clouds as a college student reached the lake before his cousin. He was the family athlete, unlike his scrawny, bookish cousin.

He caught his breath as the nocturnal creatures chirped their songs. Music whispered from the open-air theater about a mile away. The performance was an old one but a ghost-month favorite. The lake conjured his mother's warning about staying away from water during this time.

His skin prickled, and he faced the trail. "Hurry up, cousin. I'm getting tired of waiting."

The wildlife went silent.

Crying pricked his ears.

A young woman in an old-fashioned robe sobbed near a log beside the lake. She wiped her tears with her long sleeve, saw the athlete, and screamed.

He calmed her and asked if she was all right.

She nodded and tucked her long black hair behind her ear. She was beautiful.

"What are you doing here beside the lake?" He stepped toward her.

Her eyes watered, and she cowered within her robe.

"Whoa," he said. "It's okay. I'm Wei."

She bowed.

"That's an old-fashioned robe you're wearing. Are you with the opera? You're pretty enough to be an actress."

Her eyes widened. "You think I'm pretty?"

He blushed. "Well, yeah. Don't others?"

She giggled and reached for him.

He held her hand. It was cold and sent a chill up his arm.

"Let's go swimming." She smiled and led Wei to the lake.

He bit his lip.

She pouted.

He followed her to the water's edge and released her hand.

She frowned.

He took off his shoes.

She smiled.

He removed his shirt and pants.

She giggled.

He reached for her.

She stepped into the water and untied her robe so it draped over her shoulders.

He admired her as her robed body slipped underwater. Her neck followed, then her smile. Her eyes loomed on the lake's surface.

Her head submerged.

He dove after her.

Air bubbles broke the surface, then stopped.

The crescent moon emerged from the clouds.

The cousin reached the lake. "Wei." He panted and coughed. "Wei?"

The lake reflected the moon.

Wei surfaced and gasped.

Wei's cousin helped him from the water. "What were you doing in the lake?"

"There was a girl. She was beautiful. She wanted to go swimming and tried to drown me."

Wei's cousin pulled the chain around his neck, lifting a small amulet from his shirt.

"What's that?" Wei said.

"I don't know. Dad gave it to me. It's supposed to scare away ghosts."

The cousins studied the amulet.

"So." Wei raised an eyebrow. "What's supposed to happen?"

"I don't know." The cousin pressed the amulet against Wei's skin a few times.

Wei rolled his eyes and hit the amulet away. "Okay, guess I'm fine. Come on, I'm getting hungry."

Wei dressed, and the cousins left.

The lakeside insects resumed their songs. A woman's crying silenced them.

JAPAN'S OBON FESTIVAL

S IMILAR TO OTHER CULTURES, Obon is a time of ancestor worship and remembrance. Sometimes Obon's honorific *O* is dropped, and the festival is referred to as Bon.

Japan's regions may celebrate Obon differently and on different days, but the festival has three parts, which last three or four days.

The first part involves cleaning the family's grave and returning home with lanterns to guide the spirits or have a bonfire in front of the house.

For the second part, families visit shrines or temples. They have a vegetarian lunch while sharing stories of departed loved ones whose spirits are visiting them. The Bon Odori, or Bon dance, occurs at night. People dance in a large circle with their ancestors' spirits. Ghost stories are shared to prickle listeners' skins and cool them from the hot nights.

The third part involves floating lanterns in streams or rivers to guide their loved ones back to the spirit realm.

THE SORROWFUL VICTIM—OIWA
Inspired by folklore

A beautiful woman named Oiwa was beloved by all and always received compliments for her luxurious hair. She was married to a masterless samurai, or ronin, who'd accrue gambling debt and rely on Oiwa's father to bail him out.

The birds chirped as he waited in his father-in-law's manicured garden while his father-in-law talked with someone beside the koi pond.

Oiwa's father reddened, and he faced the man. "I forbid you marrying my youngest daughter. She's promised to Yomoshichi, and I know you're a criminal. Now go and don't come back."

A retainer escorted the criminal toward the ronin, and the criminal stomped away.

The retainer bowed to the ronin. "He will see you now."

The ronin hurried to his father-in-law, who fanned his reddened face.

"Good afternoon, Father."

"This better not be about money." His father-in-law panted. "I'm in no mood to discuss such things."

"But this time is different."

The father-in-law threw his fan. "Did you not hear me?"

"But Father—"

"You've pushed me too far." The red-faced man wheezed. "Oiwa deserves better than you. I'm ending your marriage."

The father-in-law stormed off.

Outside the property, the criminal approached the ronin.

"I heard how your father-in-law treated you. How about we make a deal? You kill him and keep your wife while I kill Yomoshichi and marry your wife's sister."

The ronin smirked. "You'll kill Yomoshichi? He's a samurai."

"We all bleed. Listen, I just want your sister-in-law. What do you say?"

The ronin knew Oiwa would inherit her father's fortune and agreed. He killed his father-in-law, claimed two bandits were the murderers, and vowed to avenge his death. He comforted his wife, Oiwa, as she mourned.

On a mountain path, the criminal waited for Yomoshichi. Footsteps pricked his ears. The lone samurai approached. His swords were secured to his robes.

The criminal sank from sight and drew a dagger.

He pounced, stabbing Yomoshichi. Sticky blood warmed the criminal's hands as he continued attacking.

Yomoshichi struggled away and fell off the cliff.

The criminal's heart pounded as he peered over the edge. Treetops below struck fear in the criminal, and he scrambled from the edge. *I stabbed him enough. He's dead.* The criminal stayed against the slope and started the long journey home to claim his bride.

Foragers at the foot of the mountain heard something roll along the mountainside bushes. They discovered Yomoshichi and took him to their nearby village. The village healer saved Yomoshichi, but the samurai needed time to recover.

Complications delayed Oiwa's inheritance and frustrated the ronin. Oiwa's mannerisms ticked at the ronin's tolerance, and he took his irritations out on their retainers.

While trying to relax outside, his neighbor, who was a wealthy doctor, approached.

"You seem stressed," the doctor said. "What's wrong?"

The ronin complained about Oiwa but stopped as the neighbor's granddaughter returned home.

She blushed, greeted the ronin, went inside, but eavesdropped on their conversation. She learned of the ronin's irritation with Oiwa and devised a plan to get him to leave Oiwa so she could marry him. The granddaughter made a face cream to tarnish Oiwa's beauty and gave it to her.

Oiwa thanked her for the cream and applied it. She thought the burning meant the cream was working, unaware it disfigured the left side of her face and made her left eye droop.

Her appearance pushed the ronin over the edge, but Oiwa was all he had and he needed her money. He confided with his neighbor.

"I'm sorry you're having such difficulty," the neighbor said. "You know, my granddaughter is in love with you, and I'd like to see both of you happy. If you weren't married, I'd offer you her and my fortune."

If the ronin caught Oiwa cheating on him, he could divorce her. He convinced a retainer infatuated with Oiwa to bed her and sent the others away so the three were alone.

The retainer entered Oiwa's chamber. "My lady, may I have a moment?"

"Yes, what is it?" Oiwa faced him.

Her grotesque appearance made him stumble back.

Oiwa didn't understand his reaction.

He showed her a mirror.

Oiwa was horrified the cream disfigured her, and she cried.

The retainer couldn't go through with the ronin's plan. He confessed everything to Oiwa and begged her forgiveness.

Oiwa's heart broke. As she combed her hair to conceal her deformed face, the comb took clumps of hair from her scalp. The hair piled at her feet until wisps of her luxurious locks remained on her pale head.

Oiwa grabbed a weapon and went to her husband but slipped and wounded herself.

The retainer retrieved the ronin and explained what happened.

The ronin discovered his bleeding wife. He smiled and killed the retainer.

Oiwa bled out, repeating her husband's name.

The ronin tied their bodies to planks and threw them into a river, claiming his retainer killed Oiwa.

The ronin moved in with his neighbor, and the doctor's granddaughter planned their wedding.

The rising sun stirred the mountain village. Yomoshichi thanked everyone who had saved him and journeyed home to search for the man who ambushed him.

The night wind rattled the criminal's shack as he yelled at his bride, Oiwa's sister, for refusing to share his bed.

Yomoshichi barged in.

The criminal paled in the shadow of the man he thought was dead. The criminal begged forgiveness and confessed everything, including the ronin killing his father-in-law.

A gust blustered through the shack.

"Yomoshichi. My betrothed," Oiwa's sister said. "Please kill me to atone for my shame."

"Shame? There's no shame." The criminal faced Yomoshichi. "Our marriage means nothing. We haven't even slept together."

"Please show kindness and kill me."

Yomoshichi drew his sword and struck her.

She fell, but Yomoshichi caught her and followed her to the ground.

She gave the criminal a bloody smile. "Husband. Oiwa and I share the same mother. But you and I share the same father. That is why I refused your bed."

The criminal's mouth gaped. He dropped to his knees.

Her teary eyes rolled to Yomoshichi. "You and my father were the only good men I knew. I hope you forgive my foolishness and that my father's spirit finds peace for not being avenged."

She died in her betrothed's arms.

"Yomoshichi," the criminal whispered. "Please kill me. I cannot live with this shame."

Yomoshichi held his betrothed's body and killed the criminal. The samurai, left with his betrothed, arranged a proper burial for her and went to find the ronin.

As the ronin and his new bride enjoyed their wedding night, a chill permeated the room, and his new bride's face became Oiwa.

The startled ronin killed her. But Oiwa's spirit revealed he killed his new bride.

Their commotion woke the household. The doctor entered their room.

Oiwa's spirit caused the ronin to see the doctor as the retainer he framed and killed.

The ronin killed the doctor.

The household servants entered the bedroom.

The hallucinating ronin saw them as people he killed. He murdered the servants and fled into the street.

Oiwa's ghost chipped away at his sanity and appeared in the objects he passed.

The ronin attacked some items but fled from the rest.

Yomoshichi arrived in the panic-stricken streets and grabbed a bystander. "What's going on?"

"Someone with a bloody sword is attacking objects," the bystander said. "He fled to the hills. But I'm leaving in case he returns."

Yomoshichi followed the ronin's trail of destruction.

Several days later, he found the ronin. Oiwa's haunting had made her ex-husband a malnourished lunatic who saw the people he killed in the forest trees and the food he tried to eat.

Yomoshichi pitied the ronin and ended his life.

Story Notes:

The story originated as the 1825 kabuki play *Yotsuya Kaidan*, or Yotsuya's (a neighborhood in Japan) ghost story. It was written by Tsuruya Nanboku IV. He included the real-life event of a samurai, who after learning of the affair between his concubine and servant, attached them to a board and threw them into Tokyo's Kanda River.

Many applauded how Tsuruya Nanboku turned Oiwa's sensual hair-combing into a horrific scene. Horror films and TV shows deform the left side of their characters' faces in homage to Oiwa.

Productions reproducing Oiwa's story have experienced unusual accidents and deaths. Women playing Oiwa were usually the hardest hit, causing many to compare Oiwa's story with *Macbeth*. Casts and crews usually visit Oiwa's grave to ask her permission before their productions.

Oiwa was believed to have passed on February 22, 1636, and is buried at a Tokyo temple.

THE HUNGRY GHOST FESTIVAL

THE HUNGRY GHOST FESTIVAL is a Buddhist and Taoist festival usually celebrated on the fifteenth day of the seventh lunar month. This is a period of ancestral veneration, when hungry spirits visit their families for food. Ghost money, or "joss paper," and symbolic items are burned for the spirits while rituals transmute their suffering. It is believed to have been started by the Buddhist monk Mulian.

MULIAN RESCUES HIS MOTHER
Inspired by folklore

Mulian was one of Buddha's closest disciples, gifted with supernatural powers. He teleported to heaven to see his parents but only found his father.

Dread filled Mulian as he raced into hell and found his mother's emaciated spirit. He offered food to her, but it burst into flames.

He returned to our realm and asked Buddha for help.

Buddha nodded. "On the fifteenth day of the seventh month, give offerings and feed other Buddhist monks. They will transfer your merit to your mother."

He did, and his mother's spirit ascended to heaven. As she did, Mulian witnessed all the sacrifices she had made for him. Filled with gratitude, Mulian danced for joy.

Story Notes:

Before this story, Buddhism was under fire for not honoring one's ancestors. Mulian's story proved Buddhism encouraged ancestor veneration, and his dancing with joy inspired the Japanese Bon Odori or Bon dance.

THE VENGEFUL MINISTER DU-BO
Inspired by folklore

Around 786 BCE, during China's Zhou Dynasty, a minister named Du-Bo disagreed with his emperor, Xuan. The ruthless emperor compiled false charges against Du-Bo and sentenced him to death.

As the emperor oversaw Du-Bo's execution, the minister vowed revenge for his wrongful accusation.

The impassive emperor watched Du-Bo's death.

Three years later, the emperor and his guards entered a lantern-lit chamber. Several lords greeted him, but a shrouded attendee seemed out of place.

The emperor ordered the mysterious lord to identify himself.

The lanterns flickered.

The emperor yelled at the stranger for disobeying his imperial order. His guards approached the stranger.

The lanterns dimmed as the stranger stood. His cloak dropped, revealing Du-Bo's translucent specter armed with a bow and arrow.

The guards backed into each other, and the lords paled.

"You're dead." The emperor scurried against the wall. "I killed you."

The specter raised his bow.

"Guards. Kill him."

The specter set his arrow.

The guards stepped away.

"Du-Bo." The emperor wept. "I'm sorry. I confess to framing you. Please don't kill me. We can make a deal."

The specter's arrow pierced the air and plunged into the emperor. The room gasped as Du-Bo's specter faded with the emperor's life.

Story Notes:

Du-Bo's story is one of China's shared paranormal encounters. Chinese philosopher Mozi recorded it and believed it was real because of the witnesses present.

HEIBAI WUCHANG
CHINA'S GRIM REAPERS

THE GOD OF HELL, King Yama, has two grim reapers, one black and one white. Fan Wujiu, a darker-skinned, black-robed entity, is pushy and coarse. His name translates to "those who commit crimes will have no salvation." Xie Bi'an is his pale-skinned, white-robed counterpart. He has a long tongue, kind demeanor, and his name translates to "those who make amends will be at peace." They are Heibai Wuchang, which translates to "black and white impermanence."

Heibai Wuchang collect souls and are the guardians of the underworld who enforce hell's rules upon its inhabitants. Temples are dedicated to Heibai Wuchang, and people pray to them for luck and fortune.

DEVOTED FRIENDS
Inspired by folklore

In times past, there were two officers, Fan Wujiu and Xie Bi'an. They were like brothers, but while escorting a prisoner through a forest, the prisoner escaped.

The officers split up to capture him and agreed to meet at a nearby bridge before sunset. They stressed meeting under the bridge in case the prisoner was using the road.

The stout Fan Wujiu was unsuccessful and waited under the bridge.

The tall and lean Xie Bi'an pursued their prisoner, but a storm developed. Landslides occurred around Xie Bi'an. He lost the prisoner and hurried to the bridge.

The river under the bridge surged.

Fan Wujiu scrambled for the road, but the muddy slope was too slick.

Xie Bi'an struggled through the forest. The bridge brought a smile to his face, but Fan Wujiu's drowned corpse floated past. Xie Bi'an cried. His delay killed his partner. He hung himself for atonement.

The heavenly Jade Emperor saw the devoted officers' actions and enlisted them in the afterlife.

Fan Wujiu's dark skin is from his drowning, while Xie Bi'an's pale skin and long tongue are from his hanging.

GOOD INTENTIONS
Inspired by folklore

A respected businessman owned most of the town, but his daughter was his greatest love. Smallpox almost killed her but scarred her beautiful face. She tried overcoming her disfigurement, but her confidence was shot. Her father was worried about her future and asked a servant to marry her.

The servant knew he'd inherit the father's wealth and agreed.

The daughter was happy and had two children. But when her father's health deteriorated, her husband began spending his future inheritance in gambling halls and brothels.

She visited her father every day. She asked her husband to join her, but he always said he was too tired. When she returned, he'd ask how bad her father looked, then leave for another night of debauchery.

One night, she pleaded with her husband to stay home with their family.

He stood in the doorway. "Why would I do that? I despise our family and your ugly, scarred face."

She stared at the empty doorway till the candles ran low.

"My beautiful daughter," her teary-eyed father wheezed. "Please forgive me for choosing a horrible man for you."

"Father, there is nothing to forgive. You are not to blame." She kissed his hand.

"I wish," he wheezed, "there was some way to take it all back."

She pressed her cheek against his hand to hide her tears. She smiled and stood. "I'm sorry. I must leave to start dinner, but I'll see you tomorrow." She kissed his forehead.

"Farewell, my beautiful daughter."

She bowed and left.

Tears stung her tired eyes as she hurried to the street corner, dreading her father might hear her crying. Her vision blurred. She forced her feet to move, but it felt like weights held them. She fell sobbing in the dirt.

"Miss? What's wrong?" A fair-skinned man in white robes crouched beside her.

She smiled to shore up her emotions, but her sobbing continued.

The white-robed man helped her aside.

She blubbered about her dying father, how the smallpox scarring made her childhood difficult, the love she had for her children, and the cruelty of her husband.

The white-robed man frowned and lowered his head. "I'm sorry you endured so much."

"I'm sorry for troubling you. Thank you for listening, but I need to get to the market, then return home to start dinner." She wiped her tired eyes, bowed to the white-robed man, and hurried to the market.

When she was out of sight, the white-robed man resumed his journey to her ailing father.

The crowded market gave her a headache. The walk home provided peace, but men waited beside her door. They demanded payment for her husband's gambling. She gave them all her money, but it wasn't enough.

"I'll get the rest from my father tomorrow."

One of them grabbed her hair. "How about you pay us another way?"

A boy who worked for her father approached.

The collector released her. "You better have our money tomorrow." The men left.

The boy told her that her father had died.

She held back tears and thanked him. When he was a few houses away, she stumbled into her home and cried. She wailed over losing her father and a future ruled by her unloving husband. But there was a way out. She picked up a pile of coiled rope. Looped it around a rafter. Wiped her face a few times, then admired the noose she made.

It brushed her cheek and whispered its dire promise while resting against her jaw.

She smiled.

Her door flung open.

The white-robed man entered with her children.

"Mommy. What are you doing?"

"Nothing." She left the noose, embraced her children, and sobbed.

"Your children need you," the white-robed man said.

She nodded. "Thank you."

"You may thank me by starting a new life at the river village. Gather your belongings and leave before your husband finds out."

The woman nodded. They got their things and joined the white-robed man.

He faced the road to the village with glowing eyes. "The way is clear."

The woman trembled.

His glowing eyes faded. "Don't be afraid. Your father wanted you to have this." He handed her a small fortune.

She bowed to him and guided her children to the village.

When they were out of sight, cheering erupted from the town's bar. Her husband lined up a bottle for every building he'd inherit and drank.

"Is something burning?" one of his women said.

An inferno illuminated the night. It devoured buildings in minutes but seemed to attack only certain structures.

"It consumed your house," a woman told him. "Was your family home?"

His eyes glazed as the mysterious fire destroyed his buildings.

His family were the only casualties. His fortune was lost, and he faced a mountain of debt.

The river village people loved their new resident, whose scarred face was eclipsed by her incredible smile, joyful personality, and love for her two amazing children.

RIINA

THE MELANESIAN FEMALE GHOSTBUSTER

RIINA WAS A GREAT Melanesian warrior who led her band of female warriors from the island of Lumalao. Lumalao could be a fictitious place or an old name for an island near the Solomon Islands.

Riina and her warriors might have possessed the rare Melanesians non-Caucasian gene, which grants them Caucasian features.

Riina was physically strong, knowledgeable in sacred ways, proficient in warfare, and favored using a boomerang.

THE MYSTERIOUS FEMALE WARRIORS
Inspired by folklore

Ages ago, two ghosts who ate humans kidnapped two Melanesian women. The women's husbands were artisans and offered lavish rewards to anyone who rescued their wives. Warriors attempted the task but never returned.

"Where are our great champions like Maui?" the husbands cried. "Where are our heroes?"

A group of women warriors entered the ocean-side village.

The palm trees rustled as the villagers stood between their children and the women.

"I am Riina." A warrior adjusted her armband and gestured to her group. "We are here to rescue the stolen wives."

One of the husbands approached. "Riina of Lumalao?"

She bowed. "I never liked formalities."

Riina's warriors also bowed.

Ocean waves hushed over the sand. Laughter surrounded the warriors.

The laughing villagers wiped away tears.

Riina stood and growled.

Several men mocked the warriors.

A warrior lunged for them. Riina restrained her.

The villagers fell, laughing.

Riina's eyes narrowed upon the husbands. "Your reward was for anyone. We are here to claim it."

Laughter drowned her words.

"We need to know where the ghosts took your women."

"Go back to your husbands," one of the village women said.

"Sisters..." Riina's voice trembled.

The village woman laughed along with their men.

Riina's face warmed, and her shoulders slunk.

A wide-eyed little girl among the raucous villagers pointed to the horizon.

Riina faced one of her warriors.

"I see her," the warrior said. "An unknown island lies there."

"Unknown?" Riina raised an eyebrow.

Her warrior nodded. "Beings more powerful than ghosts are said to lurk there."

"Ghosts always hide. Whether it's from us or monsters."

"Indeed."

Riina stepped toward the little girl, and the village hushed. "Thank you, little one."

The little girl's eyes glistened, and her mouth dropped open.

Riina smiled and faced her warriors. "We leave at once."

Her warriors raced to their canoe.

"Just go home and leave this to men," a village woman said.

Riina's brow furrowed. "Mark my words, villagers. I, Riina of Lumalao, am stronger than any male ghosts, and I will break them."

"The best men from across the sea never returned." The village elder scoffed. "I'm sure Maui himself would fail. What makes you think you're better?"

Riina smirked. "Because women are better warriors."

Waves crashed against Riina's canoe as her warriors sailed to the island. Riina fidgeted with her armband and brooded over the village's mocking. Her warriors talked to lighten the mood. A sound pricked Riina's ears and silenced her warrior's chatter.

The sound was wind going through a ghost's hair, and it increased.

"Hide," Riina said. "It might not be the one we're after."

Her warriors were out of sight before she finished her sentence. Riina squinted against the sun while scanning the unobstructed horizon.

Swells lapped against her canoe.

A Melanesian ghost who could lead a royal guard approached from the sky.

Riina widened her stance.

The ghost drew a red stone axe and dove toward the statuesque Riina. He yelled. His red betel-nut-stained teeth matched his axe. He drew his weapon back and swung at Riina.

She dodged him, grabbed his hair, and slammed him onto the canoe's deck.

The ghost reached for his axe, but Riina pinned him.

Her warriors leaped from hiding and tied him down.

The ghost gnashed his stained red teeth. "Release me."

Riina leaned into him. "Are you one of the ghosts who kidnapped the women?"

He laughed. "You're more of the fools trying to rescue them."

"Are they safe?"

"Of course. My brother and I would never spoil the bait providing such delicious meals."

"Where on the island are you keeping them?"

The ghost's laughter echoed the villager's laughter. His enchanted red axe glowed.

Riina left the tied ghost and stepped over his axe.

The ghost screamed as his axe's magic brilliance dimmed. He squirmed, but the warrior's bindings held.

"You wretched, worthless women. My brother will kill you. He'll slaughter all of you."

"Where is he?"

"In a mountain cave you can see from the beach. Follow the direction I came from."

"The wives?"

"They're there." The ghost frothed. "But you'll never see them. My brother will make quick work of you and devour you like those before."

Riina killed the ghost. She smiled and sighed as his body dissipated in the ocean breeze.

A warrior took her aside. "We could've tortured him."

"He wasn't worth it." Riina faced the beach. "We're burning daylight."

The current and tide aided their voyage. The cave was easy to spot, and Riina led her warriors into the ghostly dwelling.

Decay and death's stench greeted the warriors as the cave consumed the daylight.

Illumination trickled from deeper in the cave. The warriors readied themselves as they followed the light.

The cave opened to a chamber. The two wives sat beside a fire.

The wives greeted them. "Welcome. Why are you dressed as warriors instead of prisoners?"

"Sisters," Riina said. "We're here to rescue you."

The wives chuckled.

Riina contained her anger.

One of her warriors asked the wives if they were all right.

"Yes, we're fine," they said. "The ghosts provided great food and never human flesh."

Riina's eyes widened. "This is another trap."

The second ghost lunged from the darkness at the warriors, but they dodged him.

"Is everyone all right?" Riina's eyes struggled to adjust from the fire to the darkness. "Where is he?"

The ghost charged from behind her.

Air rushing through his hair pricked Riina's ears.

She pivoted and hurled her boomerang at him.

The boomerang cracked the ghost's head. The impact shattered the air and echoed throughout the cave.

Riina adjusted her armband as the ghostly remains diffused into the cave's decayed stench.

The warriors left with the wives and sealed the cave, hoping it'd provide rest to the warriors who perished before them.

Riina returned the wives to their village. The villagers were ashamed to have mocked them. The warriors forgave them. The husbands offered a larger reward, but Riina declined it because it was not part of the deal.

While the warriors loaded the riches onto their canoe, Riina noticed the little girl who helped them peek from behind a tree.

Riina called for her.

She ran to them.

Her parents watched from the tree line as their giggling daughter was embraced by the warriors.

She hushed as Riina approached.

"You helped us save those women. We are indebted to you, little sister."

The child's eyes watered, and each warrior gifted her with a weapon or piece of their attire.

Riina scanned the patchwork girl. The warrior removed her armband and tied it to the child. "Wherever you journey, we will always be with you."

The girl beamed as she rejoined her family, then waved as Riina and her warriors sailed away.

PRINCESS LEUTOGI

SOMOA'S GODDESS OF BATS & FERTILITY

THE MISTREATED PRINCESS
Inspired by folklore

WHEN TONGA AND SAMOA were at war, peace was attempted with the marriage of Tonga's king and a Samoan princess. Her name was Leutogitupa'itea, or Leutogi. Leutogi would be his second wife, and she hated leaving her beloved Samoa.

Fighting resumed between Tonga and Samoa, but Leutogi was stuck in Tonga. She was resented by her husband; his wife, the queen; and the court, who viewed her kind heart as a weakness. But the young prince was the worst. He threw things at Leutogi and called her names. Everyone encouraged the prince to avoid being his next target.

The village followed the court, and everyone mistreated the princess, including her retainer.

When she avoided the village and spent her days exploring Tonga's beauty with her mocking retainer, the queen claimed the princess's absence was an example of her laziness.

Leutogi didn't care and continued her peaceful walks.

One day, she found a fruit bat with an injured wing. She pitied the terrified animal.

Her mocking retainer shoved her aside to kill it.

Her eyes flashed, and she ordered him to stand down.

He gritted his teeth and obeyed.

Leutogi picked up the bat. "I'll comfort you, and together we won't be alone."

She returned to the palace, and everyone mocked her.

The princess ignored them and cared for her bat.

At night, Leutogi enjoyed the cool air with her bat on her lap. She fed it mango, guava, and papaya. She loved the stars, but the northern ones over her beloved island made her frown.

"I'll probably never see Samoa again."

She wept, but her bat's wiggling nose as it munched the sweet fruit made her smile. She told her bat about her beautiful Samoa, shared her people's stories, and sang their songs.

The bat's wing healed, and Leutogi knew it was time to say goodbye. She braved the forest's wrathful night spirits until she found a safe place for her bat.

Its eyes, expecting its sweet dinner, broke her heart.

She wiped her tears. "There are no stories tonight, little one. And you must find your own food."

She lifted her hands, and her bat flapped away.

"Goodbye, little one." Leutogi waited till her bat was gone, wiped her flowing tears, and went to her hut.

Leutogi's loneliness slumped her shoulders and shrank her appetite. But she hid her feelings from her unloving king and his court.

"You've hardly eaten over the past few days," the queen said during breakfast. "Is our food not good enough for you?"

"No." Leutogi grabbed more food. "I must be snacking too much."

"I haven't seen that bat of yours."

Leutogi stared at her fruit. "It healed and is back in the forest."

The queen chomped her food. It coated her tongue and ran down her mouth. "Since you have a way with little things, I'm putting you in charge of the prince. Perhaps you may tame him."

Leutogi paled and lowered her head. "Very well."

She joined the prince in his hut. They placed her bed beside his, and the queen announced Leutogi was at his beck and call.

The prince tormented Leutogi during the day, and his snoring kept her up at night. Fed up, she went into the forest, not caring about the night spirits because they couldn't be worse than the royal family and village.

Near the island's coast, something flapped beside her.

It was her bat.

The princess cried with joy, then sang and told it stories.

Leutogi's days with the tormenting prince were tolerable because her nights were with her bat.

She took her bat the finest fruit and looked forward to seeing it flap to her. Leutogi's bat brought other bats to enjoy her sweet food, stories, and songs.

Days later, Leutogi woke and discovered the prince was pale.

She asked if he was all right.

"How dare you speak to your master like that?" the prince wheezed. "I'm fine."

But Leutogi was concerned. His condition worsened, and she suggested they see his mother, the queen.

He refused.

Leutogi went to the queen, but she was busy until after dinner.

She tried caring for the prince, but he refused her and went to bed early.

After dinner, Leutogi saw the queen.

The queen's eyes narrowed. "What is it?"

The princess bowed. "It's your son—"

"The prince is your responsibility." The queen's retainers escorted Leutogi out.

The princess's shouts fell on deaf ears.

Leutogi went to her bats, who welcomed her. She cried to them and wished she had a caring family.

Screaming pricked her ears. It came from the village, and she ran back. Retainers yelled that a sickness had killed the prince.

Leutogi was blamed for neglecting him and leaving his side.

The king ordered her burned so she could feel his rage.

The princess tried explaining herself, but everyone ignored her.

Leutogi cried as they tied her to a tree and built a fire around her.

While flames warmed her skin.

She faced the northern stars and sang.

Smoke blocked the stars.

An eerie sound froze the villagers. Bats swooped upon them. The villagers scattered as the swarm extinguished the fire, and the fearful people watched the unscathed princess walk over the glowing embers from the tree.

"She's not normal," they whispered.

"Send that wretch back to Samoa to be with her own kind," the queen hissed.

"No." The king quivered. "That will make us look weak. Exile her to the offshore island. She'll die in a week on that barren rock, and we'll intercept anyone who approaches."

The king's men obeyed.

As Tonga and Samoa's war continued, the Tongan king sent Leutogi's retainer to collect her body.

The strong current delayed him. He scanned the desolate island's beach, but the setting sun provided little light. He turned to leave, but a woman called his name.

The princess greeted him and smiled. She was healthier and more beautiful than he remembered.

Leutogi's hands went behind her back. "Welcome to my island. I hear the current can be treacherous. Would you like some food or water?"

"No. Thank you." His voice trembled as he scanned the harsh and barren surroundings.

"How about some fruit?" Leutogi produced pieces of luscious papaya.

The parched-mouthed retainer stepped back. "Where'd you get that from?"

Leutogi giggled and pointed to the sky.

The retainer fell back into his canoe.

She laughed as he fumbled with his paddle and left the island.

The wind carried her laughter. It stopped when he cleared the breakers.

An eerie sound drowned out the waves sloshing against his canoe.

A cloud of bats blocked the setting sun and converged upon the island.

Leutogi welcomed them as they offered food to their princess.

Leutogi's bat settled in her lap. She fed it pieces of the papaya she offered her retainer as the swarm settled around her.

The princess smiled at her little ones. "Here's tonight's story. During a time of war between Tonga and Samoa, peace was attempted with the marriage of Tonga's king and a Samoan princess."

Story Notes:

As of this writing, the Tonga and Samoan feud has lessened, but it is so old no one recalls how or when it started.

The location of Leutogi's island remains unknown.

HINA
THE PACIFIC MOON GODDESS

The goddess Hina is shared throughout Pacific cultures, which caused her stories to be altered and letters of her name dropped or changed to Ina or Sina. She was skilled in ancient ways, and thunder and lightning filled the sky when she made the land's softest cloth.

While Pacific culture names are generally unisex, Hina is one of the few female names and given to powerful women. Madam Pele has been referred to as Hina Ke Ahi (powerful woman of fire). Hina also refers to the moon (Ma-hina or Ma-Sina). Mahina is also Hawaiian for month because Hawaiians followed a lunar calendar.

Some cultures, like the Māoris, have two Hinas. The fair Hinatea was the full moon, and Hinauri was the dark new moon.

Hinauri darkened because her brother Maui turned her husband into a dog.

Stories cast Hina as Maui's sister or mother. Which could have been because of Hina being a popular name, or the storyteller's choice.

THE DARK MAIDEN
Inspired by folklore

A beautiful woman, weary of fighting depression, threw herself into the ocean. She didn't die, and the tides took her to the sacred island of Motutapu. Its people accepted the woman, but her dark mood remained. The god of fish was taken by her, and he proposed.

She accepted but wasn't his only wife.

His other wives were jealous and attacked her to diminish her beauty, but she used her supernatural abilities to kill them and became the god's only wife.

HINA'S ESCAPE
Inspired by folklore

Wise Hina grew tired of her troublesome children and belittling husband. She searched for a peaceful place to make her fine cloth and found a rainbow path to the sun.

"Living on the sun would dry my cloth faster."

She watched the sunset, gathered her sacred items, and started on the heavenly path to catch the sun as it rose.

When it did, the sun was too hot, and it exhausted her.

She returned home and rested.

The full moon woke her. "The moon is cooler than the sun, but my cloths will still dry."

Hina gathered her sacred items. Excitement fueled her exhausted body as she lumbered on the heavenly path toward the moon.

"Come back, you worthless good-for-nothing." Her husband ran to her from their village.

Hina hurried to move her sluggish body.

Her husband's footfalls shook the rainbow path.

Hina willed her shuffling feet to go faster, but the path faded.

She leaped for the moon.

The heavens embraced her and pulled Hina to her new home.

A hand grabbed her ankle.

"You pathetic worm." Her husband panted as his free hand overlapped his grip on her ankle. "You'll never leave me."

Hina descended. Her welling tears blurred the moon.

Her husband laughed. "I'm going to break your legs when we get back so you'll crawl around like the pathetic worm you are."

"I'm a goddess." The tearful wife kicked her foot off.

Her husband fell with her foot to their village.

Hina ascended to the moon, but she was too weak to complete her journey. She chanted her strongest incantation, and the hands of night and darkness took her as far as they could, but she needed to finish the journey on her own.

Bleary-eyed, Hina swayed, keeping her balance on one foot. She couldn't do another spell to help her or grow a new foot. The final distance would be easier if she crawled.

Her husband's mocking plagued her senses.

"A goddess doesn't crawl," she snarled.

Hate fueled Hina, and she lumbered into her new dwelling.

On full moon nights, you can see Hina surrounded by her sacred belongings, joyfully making cloths for the gods.

ADI-MAILAGU
FIJI'S DARK SKY GODDESS

ADI-MAILAGU IS AN EVIL goddess who steals souls and consumes shadows. She appears as a beautiful maiden who seduces men or steals children's shadows and lives in an ivi tree. When a shadow is eaten, its owner becomes sick and dies. She also appears as a large gray rat or a crone, who harms those she doesn't like.

Offerings are made to ensure safe passage through her jungle, while her followers bathe and massage rats with oil to gain her favor.

BANISHED
Inspired by folklore

Her fall seemed an eternity. The pain of being exiled from the sky realm eclipsed the demigod Tuilakemba's injuries. Wind stung her teary eyes as she took in every detail of her beloved realm until it went out of sight.

Her splashdown created a pillar of water she wished would touch her realm. The freshwater meant she landed in a lake or river instead of the ocean.

Her eyes narrowed. *Mortals. No doubt they saw the splash. I should destroy all of them. That will teach the gods. But I'm weak.*

She changed into a large gray rat, surfaced, and scurried into the jungle. *I'll bide my time and show them all.*

THE PESKY FOLLOWER
Inspired by folklore

A man placed his offerings at Adi-mailagu's ivi tree.

The goddess became a crone and hobbled to him. "What is it?"

The man fell to the ground and bowed. "Oh, great Adi-mailagu. I seek your counsel." He listed his ancestral line.

The goddess rolled her eyes. *He's shown up every day asking how to be a better father and husband.* "Yes, yes, yes. What do you want?" She interrupted him.

He went to stand.

The goddess's eyes narrowed.

He remained on the ground. "My beloved daughter is sick. What must I do to cure her?"

The goddess sighed. *This is beneath me. I should kill these mortals.* Her ravenous soul moved her eyes to the offering. "Your offering is acceptable."

The man smiled.

Perhaps I can be rid of this mortal for at least a few days. "It's wise you came to me. Your daughter is gravely ill."

"She is?"

"Yes. Is her skin blue?"

"Um. No."

"Then you haven't much time. Gather water from a river on the far side of the island and give it to her before tomorrow's sunrise." The goddess smiled. *That should keep him busy.*

"The river you speak of flows into the ocean." He raised an eyebrow. "So shouldn't the water's healing enhance the fish we eat? Which would heal my daughter?"

The goddess's eyes flashed.

He bowed.

"What are you waiting for?" The goddess loomed over him. "Go."

He scurried into the jungle.

The goddess shook her head.

Wind rustled the overhead branches.

He returned.

She glared at him as he ran toward the river.

The goddess sighed, collected her offering, and entered her tree. She retrieved a basket overflowing with children's shadows. But she couldn't identify her follower's daughter.

She kicked the basket over.

The shadows left as the hag chewed on the tasteless offering.

Men's voices pricked her ears.

She smoothed her wrinkles, and her scraggly hair became luxurious as she shifted into a beautiful nymph. The goddess ran to the voices, hoping they didn't have any offerings.

NOPPERA-BŌ
JAPAN'S FACELESS GHOST

T HE NOPPERA-BŌ IS A non-dangerous ghost who just wants to scare people, or a disguised magical fox, or a tanuki. Disguised creatures can be identified by hair protruding from their Noppera-bō costume.

In Hawaiʻi, a 1959 *Honolulu Advertiser* newspaper article reported a Noppera-bō, who was called a Mujina, was witnessed at Oʻahu's Waiʻalae Drive-In Theater. Since then, Hawaiʻi's locals called the Noppera-bō a Mujina, and she's become a beloved entity.

The drive-in theater has closed down, but witnesses claim the Mujina moved to the shopping mall across the street.

THE NIGHT SOBA MERCHANT
Inspired by folklore

A soba merchant pushed his cart along Japan's moonlit road. "Soba, soba."

The night wind carried his voice to a traveler, who salivated, thinking of tasty noodles.

A crying woman pricked the traveler's ears. He followed the distressed sounds and found a crying woman kneeling beside the dark road.

"What's wrong?" the traveler said. "Are you hurt?"

The woman faced him. She had no eyes, no nose, and no mouth.

The traveler screamed and ran to the soba merchant. "There's a faceless woman beside the road."

"That's odd," the merchant said. "Did she look like this?" The merchant wiped his face and had no eyes, no nose, and no mouth.

THE NIGHT FISHERMAN
Inspired by folklore

A fisherman gathered his things for a perfect night of fishing.

His wife entered the room. "Please don't go. It doesn't feel right. I don't feel right."

He smirked, grabbed his things, and left.

Near Heian-kyō palace, fish jumped in the sacred imperial pond, wind blew through the graveyard beside it, and the road to his usual fishing spot seemed miles away.

He stopped, made sure no one was around, and crept to the pond beside the graves.

While readying his gear, something flashed from the corner of his eye.

A woman in a white kimono loomed beside him.

He jumped back. Then yelled at her for scaring him.

"Please don't fish here," she said.

"I'll be all right." He shooed her away. "Go home."

She smiled and wiped her face. She had no eyes, no nose, and no mouth.

He screamed, ran home, and dragged a table to barricade the door.

"What happened?" his wife said behind him.

"A faceless woman. I saw a faceless woman at the imperial pond."

She took his side. "Did she look like this?" His wife smiled and wiped her face away.

HAWAI‘I'S FAMOUS HAUNTED HOUSE

S OMEWHERE IN O‘AHU'S KAIMUKI district is one of Hawai‘i's most haunted houses. Newspaper articles, police reports, and local stories about the house include families fleeing in the dead of night; a husband killing his family, then burying them in the backyard; and a heartbroken admirer who killed a lesbian couple, then committed suicide.

Many say a Japanese kasha lurks at the house. Kasha means "burning chariot," and the creature is a humanoid cat demon who takes mortal souls to hell in its fire cart. Similar to a ghoul, the kasha eats humans and lingers at funerals or cemeteries for corpses. The connection between the kasha and the Kaimuki house was lost in time.

More stories are believed to plague the house, but many believe they are not reported since it may affect the neighborhood's land value.

The house may be one of two houses. One was torn down to make way for roads. The other is in a neighborhood that's disturbed day and night by people hoping to see ghosts.

For the neighbors' peace, I recommend leaving the house alone.

THE HAUNTINGS
Inspired by documented events

In 1942, two Honolulu police officers responded to a household disturbance. A ghost attacked the family's ten-year-old boy, along with his eighteen- and twenty-year-old sisters. The victims were slapped, strangled, thrown, and levitated.

Their mother used Hawaiian customs to chase away evil spirits, but she failed.

"My husband's a kahuna. This is all his fault," she said.

After an hour and a half of paranormal attacks, the officers escorted the family to a relative's house.

Thirty years later, a police officer responded to a disturbance at the Kaimuki house.

Three girls living there frantically explained one of them felt a hand on her arm, and they all heard talking. The girls requested the officer escort them to a nearby relative's house.

The officer agreed.

The girls piled into their car's front seat, and the officer followed in his squad car.

Near an intersection, the girls pulled into a parking lot.

The middle girl seemed to struggle against an invisible strangler.

The officer opened their door and reached for her.

A large, callused hand grabbed his arm and twisted it.

The hand wasn't one of the girls'.

The officer broke free and radioed for assistance while the girl caught her breath.

Police backup arrived to find three hysterical girls, and their pale fellow officer, explaining what happened.

The new officers told everyone to follow them to the relative's house, and the attacked girl was to ride with the officers.

Their engine didn't start.

They put her in her friend's car.

The cars started, and everyone followed the girls.

Minutes later, the girl's car door swung open.

The attacked girl fell onto the road.

The police tried helping her. But they didn't know how to stop the invisible strangler.

Story Notes:

No death was reported.

HAWAIʻI'S MISSING DIVER

THE SACRIFICE

Inspired by recorded testimony

IN THE 1950S, DURING pre-statehood Hawaiʻi, military friends swam in an Oʻahu pond. One slipped while diving from a waterfall, hit his head, and fell into the water. His friends swam to him, but the water was murky and they couldn't find him.

Splashing erupted nearby.

Their friend's shoulders broke the water's surface.

They swam for him, but the pond reclaimed his body.

The soldiers couldn't find their friend and went to the police.

A police sergeant familiar with drownings in the area sent divers and dredged the murky waters. The rescue team did their best but ran out of daylight.

The officers called it a day, but the diver's friends wanted to stay. The police wished them luck and took the path back to their vehicles.

The soldiers had basic supplies, set up a tent, and spent the night beside the pond.

As they settled in for the night, splashing from the pond became sloshing as something emerged from the water. It scurried into nearby bushes and dashed between trees.

Silence rang the soldiers' ears.

Something jumped over their tent and splashed into the water.

The soldiers trembled. Their breathing was less than a whisper.

Splashing became sloshing as the thing emerged from the water and repeated its movements.

While waiting for it to emerge a third time, shrieking pierced the air. The disruptive screeching conjured people being skinned or tortured.

As the sun rose, the police search team was on the trail near the pond when they ran into the terror-stricken soldiers.

As they explained their unusual experience, the police sergeant assured they were fine because the sun was up and there were more people with them.

At the pond, everyone was shocked the murky water was clear. They hurried to take advantage of this development but couldn't find the body.

The police sergeant climbed the falls. In the glass-like water, a body lay facedown on a flat rock. The sergeant barked orders, but his team couldn't see the body or rock. He guided them from his vantage point, and they found it.

They hoisted the body. When it left the water, a shock rippled through the sergeant and his team. The pond bubbled where the body exited. Something darted through the water, startling the sergeant. The water churned.

The sergeant ran to his team. "Bag the body and run."

They did and sprinted down the path. Splashing behind them roared into a tidal wave that swept them to their cars.

The sergeant wanted answers about the unusual pond. No scientist or University of Hawai'i expert could provide an explanation, but something an old Hawaiian man said rang true.

"In ancient Hawai'i, ponds contained an akua, or god, who accepted human sacrifices. The accident could have mimicked a sacrifice. Rituals lasted three days. You removed the body before the ritual was completed; this contaminated the water. The dirty water needed to be removed, which created the tidal wave."

HAWAI'I'S GREEN LADY OF WAHIAWA

WAHIAWA'S GREEN LADY LOOKS like a woman made up of moss and leaves. She steals kids, believing they are her missing children.

Her ethnicity is unknown, and some believe she is a creature similar to the Japanese Kappa instead of a ghost.

Her story varies but usually includes Wahiawa's Botanical Garden and the elementary school. But since her first appearance is unknown, these locations may have been added after they were established.

THE MOTHER
Inspired by folklore

Decades ago, a mother walked her children home from Wahiawa's Botanical Garden. She took a shortcut through a gulch, but then one of her children was missing.

She asked her other children where their sibling was.

They didn't know.

She searched but couldn't find her child.

Friends and family helped, but the setting sun stopped their search.

The frantic mother couldn't wait for tomorrow and ventured into the darkness.

Kids at a nearby elementary school talk about the latest comic book movies and watch videos on their mobile devices but avoid looking at the nearby foliage because they might see the ghost lady looking for her children.

THE DARING BOYS
Inspired by folklore

Boys clustered as they approached the tree where someone saw the Green Lady. The nearby stream's babbling dominated the lush area.

"She's not here," one said.

"Let's go to the water," another said.

Leaves floated downstream.

"I dare you to go to the water," a boy said.

"I don't want to get busted by my parents. We're not supposed to be here."

"Don't be a chicken."

He lifted his foot. His slipper trembled as he half stepped to the water. The others huddled around him.

Branches rustled overhead.

The boys continued daring each other toward the stream.

The area darkened as the muddy riverbank squished beneath their slippers.

Their breathing sharpened.

A presence loomed at the edge of their peripheral.

A boy screamed. The others screamed.

They scurried back to the tree, shoving each other not to be the last.

At the tree, a boy faced the stream and yelled.

The Green Lady on the other side of the river reached her bony fingers for them.

They ran and regrouped on the sidewalk beside the street.

Buildings, cars, and people washed them with relief.

A couple of boys cried, but the others comforted them and praised their bravery.

The friends promised not to tell their parents where they were and played at the park until the streetlights buzzed on, and they went home for dinner.

LONO
HAWAI'I'S GOD OF FERTILITY

L ONO-MAKUA, OR LONO THE Provider, is the god of fertility and food plants. He is one of Hawai'i's four major precreation gods who shaped the universe.

Hawai'i's wet months, or Makahiki, are dedicated to him. This four-month period begins when the Pleiades star cluster, or Seven Sisters, rises on the horizon at sunset.

Since Lono was a god of peace, Makahiki was a time of nonwork activities like festivals. It was forbidden for ali'i to conduct war or surf. Surfing wasn't allowed because the winter swell's monstrous waves allowed sharks to swim close to shore. Hawaiians saw this and respected it as the time when gods surfed.

Instead of fighting, warriors participated in physical sports. Some ali'i allowed warriors to throw spears at them, which they'd parry or dodge.

Games like 'ulu maika were played. 'Ulu maika involved rolling a puck-sized stone between two sticks. There were also cerebral challenges, like storytelling and remembering genealogical records.

Lono did all these things when he challenged the Hawaiians for his freedom.

LONO THE UNMATCHED
Inspired by folklore

During ancient Hawai'i, Lono sought a wife. He found a beautiful woman, took human form, and married her. However, another god tempted her. She was unfaithful, and Lono killed her.

The Hawaiians witnessed this and asked Lono for his name.

The god refused and had to earn his freedom by challenging the Hawaiians.

He traveled to all the islands, challenging anyone to any sport they named.

The Hawaiians were shocked that a stranger beat their best warriors, scholars, kahunas, and ali'i.

Lono made a final call for challengers.

The wind tossed his hair.

"I've won my freedom and must leave." Lono created a canoe the size of a city and outfitted it with the finest cloth.

"Are we to sail this for you?" the Hawaiians asked.

"I can sail this alone," Lono said.

The Hawaiians provided him with supplies.

He faced them. "I am leaving but will return."

The Hawaiians bowed as Lono sailed for Tahiti.

RAHU-KETU
THE SUN-EATING DEMON

T HE LORD OF ILLUSION, Rahu-Ketu, was a shadow demon beheaded by Vishnu while gaining immortality. While the demon was beheaded, his head and body were immortal and became Rahu and Ketu, respectively.

Rahu causes eclipses by trying to devour the sun or moon. But since he is a disembodied head, they pass through him.

Rahu is forever directly across from his body, Ketu. This transcended to Hindu astrology, which affiliates Rahu with the north and Ketu with the south.

THE DEMON OF ILLUSION
Inspired by folklore

When gods fought evil beings, there was the nectar of immortality. The gods planned on drinking the nectar to gain immortality, but demons stole it. The god Vishnu transformed into the enchanting goddess Mohini, distracted them, and reclaimed the nectar.

However, the demon Rahu-Ketu wasn't fooled. He cast an illusion disguising himself as a god and joined them.

The nectar was passed to Rahu-Ketu.

The sun and moon gods' illumination accidentally revealed Rahu-Ketu's demon form.

The gods alerted Vishnu.

Rahu-Ketu drank the nectar as Vishnu cut the demon's head off.

But the demon gained immortality. His head became Rahu and his body, Ketu.

YUKI-ONNA
JAPAN'S SNOW WOMAN

Y UKI-ONNA MEANS "SNOW WOMAN," but she is known by other names.

She is one of Japan's most famous ghosts, whose stories were estimated to have begun around the 1300s. Yuki-onna was also featured in Japan's 1964 horror film masterpiece, *Kwaidan*.

She is a beautiful, fair-skinned, blue-lipped young maiden who wears a kimono and glides across the snow. Like other Japanese ghosts, she doesn't have feet. While many consider her a ghost, some believe she is from the moon and could not find a way back.

Sometimes she has a baby, which made some believe she was a mother or pregnant when she died. She uses her baby to acquire victims by asking them to hold her child. When someone does, her baby gets heavier. The victim isn't able to move and freezes to death.

A samurai avoided this by placing a knife in his teeth before accepting the child. Yuki-onna, scared her child would be cut, refused to hand it over and rewarded the clever warrior with riches.

When Yuki-onna appears at someone's house, asking for water, she can be vengeful or merciful. Refuse her, and she will kill you. Give her water, and she may reward you. Offer her a hot beverage, and she will flee.

A MOTHER'S STRUGGLE
Inspired by folklore

A woman marched against the winter storm. She cursed how quickly it developed while her squirming baby fueled her fighting spirit.

Their village's lights glowed through the snow. She smelled the burning fires and imagined hot miso soup coating her tongue.

A flurry knocked her over.

She gripped her bundled child, and the storm devoured her.

Japan's villagers keep an eye on raging arctic storms because they might bring the snow woman, Yuki-onna.

THE SNOW WOMAN'S PROMISE
Inspired by folklore

The dark sky announced the approaching storm. A woodcutter and his apprentice hurried, securing their day's goods to make the ferry.

They raced over the hill. The river glistened, but the transport was gone.

Gusts toppled the woodcutter. The apprentice helped his master into the ferryman's decrepit storehouse and fought the howling storm to barricade the door.

The shaking shelter urged them to reinforce the door, but their drained bodies collapsed and sleep overtook them.

A chill woke the assistant. Breath vapor poured from his mouth, and a woman loomed over his master. Her long black hair draped fair skin that matched the snow-covered room. Her breath vapor fell from her blue lips onto the master. He exhaled and became motionless.

She faced the apprentice.

He yelled.

She pounced on him.

He tried to break from her, but she was too strong.

Her blue lips twisted into a smirk. "I will let you live if you promise never to tell anyone what you saw tonight. Break your word, and I will kill you. Understand?"

The assistant nodded.

The woman eased off him. A gust whipped through the shack, and she floated away.

The apprentice returned to his village, told them his master died. But didn't mention the woman.

Time passed, the apprentice became a master woodcutter, and a beautiful, fair-skinned woman joined the village. He courted her, they married, and had children. As the children grew, the villagers remarked about the fair-skinned wife's ageless beauty.

One night during a snowstorm, the woodcutter smiled at his sleeping children and joined his wife beside the fire.

"I haven't seen a storm like this since my master died," he said. "A beautiful woman killed him and would've killed me, but I promised not to tell anyone about her."

"Why do you break your word now?" His wife morphed into the woman who killed his master.

Her husband jumped back.

She reached for him.

One of their children coughed in their sleep.

Tears fell from the woman. "You promised."

"I'm sorry. It was stupid of me. I promise it won't happen again."

She wiped her tears and studied their sleeping children. "You are a good father and provider." Rage filled her teary eyes. "Promise me you'll look after our children. But if you make them unhappy, I'll return and kill you."

He nodded. "Yes, I promise."

A gust blew open the door. She sailed away while her crying echoed in the howling storm.

Story Notes:

Some renditions of this popular story end with the husband escaping death by pointing out he didn't tell anyone since Yuki-onna was his wife.

THE ARCTIC QALUPALIK

THE QALUPALIK IS A creature who kidnaps children playing near the water's edge or youngsters who misbehave. The victim's youth is drained, and they are eaten or become a Qalupalik.

Qalupalik are tall humanoid fish with scaley blue-green skin, webbed claws, sharp teeth, large eyes, and long seaweed hair. They wear an Inuit's parka with a large hood traditionally used to carry children.

A Qalupalik is near when you smell dead or rotting fish, steam rises from the water, and humming or knocking comes from the ice beneath you.

THE STRANGE FISHMAN
Inspired by folklore

Children snuck from their chores to play near the water. Intoxicated by the thrill of disobeying their parents, they played in the snow and slid on the ice.

Knocking thundered beneath the children.

Their vapored breath thickened.

Knocking rumbled between them and the water.

The wide-eyed children studied the ice.

Knocking pounded near the water's edge.

A blue-green, scaley webbed claw rose from the water. Its nails dug into the ice. Arm muscles tightened, and a Qalupalik climbed onto the ice. Water streamed from the creature's parka as it moved its seaweed hair from its black orbed eyes.

The stench of dead fish wrinkled the children's noses.

The Qalupalik approached.

They huddled together.

It eclipsed them and reached for one of their arms.

A child grabbed the others and ran.

The Qalupalik screamed. It lunged for them, missed, and slid across the ice as the children ran home.

THE ARCTIC HUNTER
Inspired by folklore

A grandmother was left to raise her grandson. She was poor and despised having another mouth to feed. Her village offered to provide for them, but the grandmother's pride almost caused the two of them to starve.

Remembering the Qalupalik stories, she encouraged her grandson to spend the day playing beside the water.

That night, she readied her meager dinner, and her grandson returned home.

She threw a spoon at him. "I told you to play beside the water."

The boy cowered in the corner. "I did, but it's too cold and dark now."

"Go back tomorrow. I don't want to see you here when the sun's out." She gave him half her meal, ate her few bites, and went to bed.

Their days continued until her grandson didn't return.

Tears blurred her vision, and she prayed for forgiveness.

Knocking on the door startled her.

"I'm sorry to disturb you," a man from her village said. "Our children saw a Qalupalik take your grandson."

She cried.

The men assured her they'd do their best to find him and left.

As the rescue party neared the village's edge, two figures approached from the vast arctic.

"Halt," a villager said. "Please state your business."

"I am a hunter." A figure stepped into the light and gestured to the other. "This is my assistant."

The assistant stepped forward. "He's not just any hunter. He's the greatest hunter around."

The hunter smirked. "Please excuse his exaggerations. A storm approaches, and we seek shelter."

The villagers mumbled.

The hunter stepped back. "We can manage if it's too much trouble."

"No, it's fine," a villager said. "We can offer shelter. We were just going to look for a missing boy."

The hunter nodded. "Where was he last seen?"

"Near the water. Children saw a Qalupalik take him."

"A Qalupalik?" The assistant beamed. "My master's hunted such creatures."

"Is this true?"

"Yes." The hunter studied the gathering clouds, then faced the villagers. "If it was a Qalupalik, it won't harm the child. It will protect him from the storm, and in exchange for shelter, we shall find him tomorrow."

The villagers accepted the two, and the storm raged through the night.

When the sun climbed blue skies, the hunter and assistant went to where the child was kidnapped.

The boy sat in the low tide shallows.

"There he is." The assistant ran for him.

The hunter grabbed the assistant's shoulder. "Something doesn't seem right." He waved to the boy.

Wind rippled the water beside the unblinking child.

The hunter tested the ice. "Be quick, but stay alert."

They raced for him.

The child's eyes widened. "Two men are approaching."

A rope of seaweed tightened around his waist and pulled him underwater.

The hunter stopped his assistant at the water's edge. "No, it's too risky. We need to tell the villagers what happened." He scanned the area and nodded toward a nearby snow dune. "We'll make camp behind that and try again tomorrow."

They woke before sunrise and hid near the shallows.

The tide lowered, revealing the child's head, shoulders, and body.

They ran for him.

The child's eyes widened. "Two men are approaching."

The seaweed rope tightened.

The hunter drew his knife, lunged, and cut the rope.

The severed end whipped into the water, and the duo helped the child onto land.

The village welcomed them back.

The boy's demeanor returned. Near his home, he talked with others.

The hunter asked the villagers to give the family some private time. When they were alone, he kneeled beside the child. "Why were you playing beside the water?"

"My grandmother told me to."

His grandmother emerged. She cried while embracing her child and welcomed the duo in.

They thanked her and entered.

She asked about their travels.

The assistant answered. But the holes in the walls, blankets, ceiling, and lack of food distracted the hunter.

"When will you be leaving?" the grandmother said.

"The area is rich with resources," the hunter said. "We may stay awhile."

His assistant did a double take.

The duo joined the village. The hunter provided for the family and trained the boy, who became one of the area's greatest hunters.

THE AURORA AUSTRALIS AND BOREALIS

T HE AURORAS ARE A natural phenomenon found in earth's northern and southern hemispheres. Aurora Borealis means morning light from the north, and Aurora Australis means morning light from the south.

Northern arctic cultures viewed the Aurora Borealis as their ancestors playing a soccer-like game with a walrus skull for a ball. Or the players were walrus or seal spirits playing with a human's skull as a ball.

Asian cultures believed the lights were fire from fighting dragons representing good and bad.

Aborigines saw Aurora Australis as a great sky war or dead spirits ascending to the heavens.

Cultures believe whistling or pointing at the Aurora Borealis is bad luck, and spirits will take you away. Many scrutinized the belief that children conceived under the lights would become intelligent and attractive.

DRAGONS' BREATH
Inspired by folklore

The white dragon winced from his injury inflicted by the dark dragon. But it now understood the dark dragon was fast, weaker, and reckless. The white dragon advanced on its opponent. It drew the dark dragon's red breath.

It missed.

The white dragon chuckled at his predictable foe and unleashed his green fire breath upon him.

Below them, Chinese villages, the emperor in his castle, and troops along the country's Great Wall enjoyed the dragons' fires igniting the sky.

THE SPOILED CHILD
Inspired by folklore

A boy complained about his parents as he struggled through mounds of snow. *I'll never get home at this rate.*

His jaw dropped. *What if I got home late? That'd make them think twice about sending me out in the snow. They'll also start asking less of me.*

He picked up a stick near skeletal trees, waved it around, and barked orders at his army of tree warriors.

When the sun lowered behind his wooded army, his stomach growled.

He frowned. *They'll really worry if I stayed longer.*

He threw his stick and plunged his hands in his pockets. Something jabbed his knuckle. It was jerky he forgot about. He giggled, ate the jerky, and watched the sunset.

While his tree warriors reported their victory, the wind whipped his clothes.

His teeth chattered. He tossed his stick and headed home.

Warmth grew within him. *My body is used to the cold.* He got his stick, resumed playing, and laughed. *My parents are going to be so mad.*

Darkness consumed him and his tree warriors. Hunger, cold, and fatigue sank their claws into the fussy, irritable child.

Pink, green, purple, and blue ribbons pierced the dark sky.

He remembered his father saying the lights were spirits dancing and playing. He frowned. The spirits were having fun, and he wasn't. He pointed, whistled, and yelled. "It's not fair you get the play while I struggle!"

He sensed a presence in the darkness.

Shadows made his warrior trees hideous creatures. He threw his stick at the tree line.

It landed beside a humanoid figure.

A chill ran through the petrified boy.

Hoping his eyes were playing tricks on him, he looked for a bush or log to be the figure.

But it was a darkened humanoid figure.

The child blinked.

The figure was gone.

The boy jolted. *I did see someone.*

A pink ribbon streaming across the sky darkened to red.

With mounting dread, he scanned the area.

The figure stood beside the trees near him.

Fear squeezed tears from the child.

He prayed for forgiveness and promised to be a good boy.

His father yelled behind him and erupted from the tree line.

The crying boy ran into his father's arms and apologized for not coming home.

The father forgave his son and carried him home.

The boy peeked over his father's shoulder.

The figure faded among the trees.

POLI‘AHU
THE HAWAIIAN SNOW GODDESS

Poli‘ahu is the Hawaiian goddess of compassion and snow. Her name means temple bosom or cloaked blossom. She is the oldest of three sisters. They all wore cloaks, were intelligent, adventurous, athletic, and attractive. But fair-skinned Poli‘ahu was one of Hawai‘i's most beautiful women, and her cloak drapes Mauna Kea with snow.

She enjoyed cliff diving and joined her sisters in he‘e holua, or sled surfing, a deadly activity of racing over snow or rocks on sleds twelve feet long and six inches wide, capable of reaching fifty miles per hour.

The sisters protect the Big Island's snow-capped dormant volcano, Mauna Kea. Mauna Kea is Poli‘ahu's temple, but she shares it with other akua, or gods, and is the resting place of ali‘i and kahunas.

Mauna Kea's Lake Waiau is the world's highest lake, and its waters are very sacred. Waiau is named after Poli‘ahu's sister, who is its protector.

While other gods demanded temples and sacrifices, Poli‘ahu requested flowers and people to care for the land. This compassion made her beloved by farmers and fishers instead of the ruling class, who preferred violent gods to aid their wars.

Many stories of Poli‘ahu and her sisters were lost since Western settlers preferred recording Hawai‘i's violent gods.

The Laupahoehoe coast resulted from Poli‘ahu and Pele's battle of ice and fire.

THE SISTERS
Inspired by folklore

After Hawai'i was formed, its beauty made the Hawaiian god Kāne weep. His tears fell on a taro plant and formed four beautiful goddesses: Poli'ahu, the fair-skinned goddess of snow whose beauty was unmatched; Lilinoe, the goddess of mist, dead fires, and desolation; Waiau, a lake goddess who protected Mauna Kea's lake, which supplies Hawai'i's most sacred water; and Kahoupokane, the goddess of Hualālai volcano and master kapa cloth maker who crafted the sister's white cloaks.

The white-cloaked sisters became Mauna Kea's protectors.

However, south of Mauna Kea is Kilauea volcano, domain of Pele, the goddess of fire, who despised Poli'ahu and her sisters.

THE WISH OF A GODDESS
Inspired by folklore

The sun rose as Poli'ahu adjusted her white cloak, sat along Mauna Kea's slopes, and gazed upon her beloved Hamakua Coast. As laughing couples played along the shore, she closed her eyes and made her usual wish.

A handsome young ali'i from Kaua'i was struck by Poli'ahu's beauty. He approached but was hesitant since gods don't associate with mortals.

But Poli'ahu enjoyed mortals and welcomed him.

They talked and played until it was time for the ali'i to leave.

He smiled at Poli'ahu. "Come with me and be my wife."

She glanced at her beloved Hamakua Coast and the squawking birds that passed. A tear trickled across her cheek, and Poli'ahu agreed.

Her sisters cried and bid farewell to their oldest sibling.

Watery-eyed Poli‘ahu tore herself from their embrace. "I leave Mauna Kea to you. Be strong, my sisters."

When Poli‘ahu and her ali‘i arrived on Kaua‘i, she discovered he was engaged to a woman from Maui.

Poli‘ahu faced her ali‘i. "What is the meaning of this?"

He smiled. "I'm going to marry both of you, and you'll be my second wife."

The ali‘i's betrothed studied Poli‘ahu and smirked. "You're not as desirable as you think."

Poli‘ahu's heart broke. She filled with rage and cast a burning frost on the couple but didn't kill them.

The woman fled to a canoe and returned to the island of Maui while the ali‘i begged Poli‘ahu to spare his life and stay with him.

"Your insulting never ends. I will spare you but not the next time we meet."

Poli‘ahu spirited herself back to Mauna Kea. Her sisters comforted the goddess, but she wanted to be alone.

The sun rose as Poli‘ahu adjusted her white cloak, sat along Mauna Kea's slopes, and gazed upon her beloved Hamakua Coast. As laughing couples played along the shore, she closed her eyes and made her usual wish.

That the right men for her and her sisters would soon appear.

THE BATTLE OF ICE & FIRE
Inspired by folklore

Poli‘ahu's friends cheered her as she sledded down Mauna Kea. The trade winds carried their revelry south to Kilauea volcano and echoed in Pele's solitary domain.

Pele gritted her teeth. "I'll prove I'm the superior god by besting Poli'ahu." The fire goddess donned her most beautiful maiden form and went to Mauna Kea.

Poli'ahu and her friends finished another race near Mauna Kea's base. The snow goddess won again, and her friends praised her unmatched sledding.

Poli'ahu blushed and raised her cloak's hood. "Mahalo."

Her friends asked how they could improve, and she helped them.

"You are making quite a racket." Pele approached.

Poli'ahu smiled, unaware the beautiful maiden was Pele. "I'm sorry. Would you like to join us?"

Pele forgot how stunning Poli'ahu was. "I'd like to," Pele stammered and cleared her throat. "But I don't have a sled."

"Please use mine," Poli'ahu said. "I'll use another."

"Your kindness is disgusting," Pele mumbled.

"I'm sorry. Did you say something?"

Pele forced a smile. "Your kindness is endearing."

"Ah, mahalo." Poli'ahu's smile was breathtaking.

Pele contained her anger and snatched Poli'ahu's sled.

Poli'ahu lifted a normal sled. "Let's go up a bit and start there."

Pele smirked. "I was thinking we start at the summit."

Poli'ahu's friends gasped.

The snow goddess leaned toward Pele. "Are you sure? That's very dangerous."

"Yes. I'm a good sledder."

"Okay. This is going to be fun." Poli'ahu gave another perfect smile and started up the slope.

Pele stomped a half step ahead of the snow goddess.

Poli'ahu's friends stayed behind and made bets on how badly the stranger would lose.

Poli'ahu made small talk with Pele.

Anger bubbled within the fire goddess as she answered in gruff, one-word bursts.

Poli‘ahu continued trying to get Pele to talk.

The fire goddess' anger festered into rage. Pele contained it by replying with nods or shaking her head.

At the summit, Poli‘ahu faced Pele. "Are you sure you want to do this?" Pele nodded.

Poli‘ahu beamed. "First to the bottom wins, okay?" Pele nodded.

Poli‘ahu adjusted her white cloak. "Ready?" Pele readied herself and nodded.

The goddesses shot down the snowy slope.

Pele took the lead with her skill and Poli‘ahu's superior sled. She chuckled, but the snow goddess appeared in her peripheral and passed.

As Poli‘ahu's lead widened, Pele clenched her teeth and summoned a tremor to jostle Poli‘ahu. But the snow goddess maintained her balance and carved a sizable lead.

Pele furrowed her brow and melted snow in Poli‘ahu's path.

But Poli‘ahu's powers restored the path without her noticing, and she barreled toward the finish line.

Pele opened a lava pit beneath Poli‘ahu.

The falling goddess grabbed her white cloak and spirited herself back to Mauna Kea's summit. She looked down upon her competitor. "Pele-honu-amea." Her voice echoed. "Goddess of fire, keeper of mighty Kilauea. You should be ashamed for dishonoring our game and disrespecting my domain with your trickery."

"She's so damn respectful." Pele reached the foot of Mauna Kea, raised lakes of lava, and sent its waves to Mauna Kea.

Poli‘ahu gasped and lowered her head. "So be it." The goddess summoned a snowstorm that hardened the lava and knocked Pele down.

Pele jumped up, summoned more lava, and threw fireballs at the snow goddess.

Poli'ahu effortlessly countered Pele's attacks, causing explosions that injured the fire goddess.

But Pele continued fighting.

Poli'ahu's eyes watered as Pele's injuries worsened. The fire goddess swayed, launching haphazard attacks until an explosion slammed her down.

A tear fell from Poli'ahu. "Pele, goddess of fire, mistress of Kilauea, you are beaten. I can kill you but do not wish such a tragedy even though you would not grant me the same mercy if our roles were reversed. Return to your domain and know you may live in peace as long as you stay away from my side of the island. Now please go."

Bleary-eyed Pele struggled to her feet. *Namaka, my own sister, killed me long ago. But am I not stronger now?* Tears covered Pele's cheeks. She screamed, unleashing more fireballs.

Poli'ahu closed her watery eyes, grabbed her white cloak to block Pele's attacks, and summoned a great wind that swept Pele's frail body to Kilauea.

Poli'ahu wiped her tears and dusted her cloak.

"Poli'ahu beat Pele," her friends cheered.

The blushing goddess joined her friends. "No one beat anyone. Pelehonuamea is a goddess who deserves our respect."

"You still beat her."

Poli'ahu retrieved her sled and grinned. "Can we please resume our games?"

The trade winds carried their revelry south to Kilauea. Pele laughed and nursed her wounds. "Fools. I'm the superior god. I beat Poli'ahu. I beat her in our sled race."

THE WENDIGO

A WENDIGO IS SOMEONE who wished to become the creature, or a human cursed by partaking in cannibalism.

Traditionally, wendigos resembled malnourished, taut-skinned humans with sunken eyes, but modern interpretations depict them as anthropomorphic creatures with animal skulls, antlers, and cloven hooves.

A wendigo's size increases after eating, causing a cycle of constant hunger, which explains why the wendigo is a metaphor for greed and excessive consumption. Western settlers' desire for land and resources reflected this, which contrasted with the indigenous people's lifestyle.

Wendigo psychosis is a condition where someone believes a wendigo spirit is possessing them. Symptoms include depression, delusion, thoughts of homicide, and cannibalism.

SNOWBOUND
Inspired by folklore

The snowstorm lashed against the dwelling as a woman gathered her family and brought their meager dinner to the table.

Her husband pried himself from the window. "I hope it lets up soon."

His daughter climbed into her seat at the table beside her brothers. "Mommy, why don't we have more food?"

"Hush now." Her mother took a breath. Her wrinkled brow smoothed. "Let's be thankful for what we have."

Her children scratched their bald spots; their taut skin slid over their collarbones.

She forced a smile as they finished their meal in a few bites.

Her husband's eyes widened. "I think it's clearing." He jumped from his chair, grabbing his coat and rifle.

She purged her mind of the wendigo stories and prayed he'd be successful.

CURSE OF THE WENDIGO
Inspired by folklore

The winter snowstorm weighed the hunter's fatigued legs. Dim lights piercing the storm's veil quickened his pulse.

A village. He laughed and fought his burning legs until he threw himself against the nearest shelter.

Its residents helped him in.

The sun greeted the villagers gathering outside the home. Their expressions matched those of the host family's children who studied the stranger. Their mother served soup to her husband and their guest.

The husband pushed back his gray hair and gestured to the crowd. "Please excuse them."

The hunter accepted his soup. "Why are they scared?"

"They fear you are wendigo," a voice hissed from the door. The village elder entered.

The wife helped him into a chair.

The elder panted. "We stopped a warrior and wife from eating their child." He nodded to the host. "His brother."

The host's wife added wood to the fire, collected the children, and left.

The firewood snapped. Embers reflected in the elder's dull eyes. "We banished them. But discovered tracks around our village that led to their dwelling in the nearby wood. See for yourself; they live as wendigos." The elder wiped a tear.

The hunter nodded. "You wish me to kill them."

The gray-haired host dropped his soup bowl.

"I am sorry," the hunter said. "I mean no disrespect. I've dealt with wendigos. There is no remedy."

The gray-haired host lowered his head.

"Please allow me a day to gain my strength," the hunter said.

His host nodded.

The following day, voices outside the shelter woke the hunter.

"Is anyone missing?" a man said.

"No," another said.

The hunter gathered his things, grabbed water, some jerky, and went outside.

Fresh wendigo snow tracks circled the village and led to the woods.

The gray-haired host glanced at the hunter's things. "You're going now?"

The hunter squinted at the dark clouds and jogged into the woods.

Hints of burning wood intensified as he crept toward a ramshackle hovel in the clearing. He hid behind bushes and watched the dwelling.

Clouds dimmed the sun.

A woman appeared in a window. Her bones slid under her taut, leathery skin. Her long nails completed her clawlike hands. Faint light glinted from her sunken eyes beneath cobwebbed hair.

The hunter ate some jerky. *Where's your husband?*

The woman toiled in the kitchen.

The sky darkened. The hunter crept toward the hovel.

Aromatic cooking greeted him as he listened at her door.

She wheezed.

He knocked.

Clatter erupted from the kitchen. Her lumbering steps approached, and the door opened.

She gave him a rotten-toothed smile. "Yes?"

"I'm sorry to disturb you. Could you offer shelter from the coming storm?"

Drool dripped from her wrinkled lips. "Yes, yes, of course. I'll get you some soup."

"Thank you."

She cackled and closed the door behind him.

The structure groaned. Holes in the roof displayed storm clouds. Wind whistled through the walls and flapped tattered animal skins. Scraps of a sleeping mat and pieces of broken chairs littered the floor.

She hurried to a cluttered table beside the stove and offered the only usable chair. "Sit. And I'll make you a bowl."

The chair squeaked as he sat. "You must be strong to live alone."

She cleared some of the table. "My husband will be home soon." A giggle erupted from her. Saliva dripped across the open space. "Are you part of the river tribe?"

The hunter's eyes widened. *There's another tribe?* He calmed himself. "Yes. Your soup smells delicious."

She cleared more of the table. "Thank you. Can you please check it to see if it's to your liking?"

He went to the pot, grabbed the ladle, and stirred the soup.

"My husband can't wait to meet you."

The ladle struck an object. A human skull surfaced and faced the hunter.

He turned to the woman.

She lunged at him with a knife.

He whacked her face with the ladle.

She recoiled.

He pressed his attack, took her knife, and killed her.

Her body collapsed beside the fireplace.

He prayed for her—and her husband's remains in the soup.

He left. Lightning shot between clouds. Darkness loomed beyond the first row of trees. Thunder rumbled as he guessed where the river tribe was and headed toward the gloom.

Howling from the dark froze his advance.

Tree limbs snapped behind him.

His skin prickled as he forced his paralyzed body to face the disruption.

A wendigo's sunken face broke through the treetops. It sniffed, faced the hovel, and wailed.

The hunter's legs buckled, and he fell against the shelter.

The wendigo erupted from the trees at him.

He rolled from the attack.

The wendigo hit the wall, part of it, and the roof collapsed.

Adrenaline conquered the hunter's fear. He unleashed a series of attacks, but they were ineffective.

The blizzard knocked him toward the tree line while the wendigo dug in against the gale.

The creature sniffed and crawled after its prey.

The hunter leaned against a tree, a shield against the blizzard, then sliced the wendigo's eye.

The creature roared, reared back, and swatted the trees, breaking them at their trunks.

The hunter stumbled to escape the rain of thorny branches tearing his back and neck. Tree trunks pummeled the earth near him. He emerged beside the beast.

The wendigo lifted its foot.

The hunter rolled. Wooden shrapnel plunged deeper into him as he left a blood trail that the creature stomped.

The wendigo roared.

The hunter laid on thorny branches. While the cold numbed his pain, a crimson path from the woods led to the wendigo's ankle, where a laceration stained the bleached ground. The hunter glanced at the row of broken trees, their jagged trunks protruding from the ground.

The area darkened. The wendigo's good foot was over him.

The hunter sprang and attacked the wendigo's injured ankle.

The creature roared, fell, and impaled itself on the broken trees. Its breathing stopped.

A flurry toppled the hunter. He scrambled from the burying snow to the hovel's collapsed wall.

The fireplace was destroyed. Snow and debris littered the floor and table. He bundled himself with the tattered animal skins. The remaining roof creaked, and he crawled under the table.

The blizzard screamed through the hovel as the dead woman's grinning face watched him fall asleep.

Pain screaming across the hunter's body woke him. His blood soaked the animal skins. Red snow surrounded him. Snow blanketed the woman and her impaled husband.

The sun illuminated the blue sky.

He tended most of his injuries and noticed the collapsed fireplace hid the soup pot.

He cleared the debris. Some embers were beside the warm pot.

The fragrant soup made his stomach growl.

Its surface reflected his dark eyes and pale face. His drool dripped and shimmered his image.

He shoved the pot, and it clanged against debris. Embers extinguished with a hiss, and bones clattered across the floor. The skull watched him lumber outside.

The river tribe was visible through the cleared trees. He used a branch as a walking stick and went to them.

They tended to him and confirmed several of their people were missing. He told them of the wendigos and the village beyond. The village welcomed the river tribe, both settlements thrived, and the hunter continued across the frozen plain.

THE BUTTERFLY LOVERS

S CHOLARS TRACED THIS STORY to around the Tang Dynasty (618–907 CE), at least nine hundred years before Shakespeare's *Romeo and Juliet*. The butterfly lovers inspired many plays, stories, and a violin concerto. China's Ningbo city has several places named after the lovers, and in October 2005, Ningbo became sister cities with Romeo and Juliet's Verona.

BEST FRIENDS
Inspired by folklore

Zhu Yingtai's wealthy father hoped her ambitions would fade and she'd become an ideal wife.

But she wanted to attend school, which was reserved for men.

She devised a plan and made her father's favorite meal.

He smiled at the food and raised an eyebrow. "What do you want?"

Zhu Yingtai's eyes widened. "Why, nothing, Father."

"We'll save a lot of time if you just told me."

Her cheeks reddened. "I want to attend the highest school in the land."

He laughed. "You're a girl."

"Yes, but I'll attend disguised as a boy."

He sipped his tea. "That may work. Let's see how long your charade lasts. But promise you'll return when I call for you."

She thanked him, and he enjoyed his meal.

At school, Zhu met the bookish Liang Shanbo. They spent hours studying, were always together, and she developed feelings for her clueless classmate.

Three years later, Zhu's father sent a letter for her to come home. He didn't mention a return date.

Zhu began walking home.

Liang couldn't part with his friend and stayed by her side.

Zhu wanted to say how her heart ached for Liang but didn't know if he saw her as a classmate or lover. "Liang, I feel we are like mandarin ducks."

His head tilted. "The love ducks? I guess."

Zhu sighed. *He didn't get it.* Her eyes widened. "Did I tell you about my sister?"

"You have a sister?"

"Yes. She's very smart, beautiful, and perfect for you. Visit me, and I'll introduce you."

Liang blushed. "Okay."

They parted after eighteen miles and counted down the days to Liang's visit.

Zhu wore her best gown to welcome Liang. She was stunning, and Liang was speechless. Zhu confessed she disguised herself as a boy to attend school, and the friends admitted their love for each other.

Liang cleared his throat. "I'm to be the magistrate of Ningbo, and I'd like you to come with me."

Zhu's eyes sparkled. A tear ran down her cheek. "Yes."

Liang asked Zhu's father to marry her and explained his role as Ningbo's magistrate would more than provide for them.

Zhu's father frowned. "You are a fine man, Liang. But she's to marry a merchant. I cannot break that agreement. I'm sorry."

The lovers' hearts broke, and they parted.

Liang sleepwalked through his days as Ningbo's magistrate. His food became bland. Tailored clothes became baggy. He became sick and passed away.

Zhu emotionlessly learned womanly duties while her fiancé complained about her distant nature.

Zhu's father entered her chamber, dismissed her retainers, and kissed his pale daughter's forehead. "Please tell me. What it will take to restore yourself?"

Life flickered in her dull eyes. "Let me see Liang in Ningbo one last time, and I'll be the most ideal wife the world's seen."

He kissed his daughter's cheek. "So be it."

Color returned to Zhu. She changed into comfortable clothes and dashed for Ningbo before her father made arrangements.

On the outskirts of Ningbo, thunder rumbled from the gathering clouds. Rain pelted Zhu. Wind whipped her clothes and shoved her several feet back down the road.

She gritted her teeth and struggled against the wind, turning her face from the stinging rain. Lightning illuminated a grave's marker beside the road. It read Liang.

She gasped.

Thunder quaked.

She approached the fresh grave. Her tears blended with the rain as her fingers traced the symbols of Liang's name. She embraced the marker, collapsed into the mud, and sobbed a prayer to join him.

"Hey!" travelers yelled from the road. "Get out of the storm."

Sheets of rain, howling winds, and slamming thunder stopped.

Zhu's skin prickled.

Lightning struck the ground beside her, opening Liang's grave.

She jumped in.

The travelers screamed and ran to her.

A sunbeam illuminated the grave. Two butterflies fluttered from the hole into the sky.

'ŌHI'A AND LEHUA

THE 'ŌHI'A LEHUA TREE, or Metrosideros polymorpha, is the scraggly tree that develops after a lava flow. This botanical anchor supports vegetation and animals and is part of the process that filters rain into drinking water.

'Ōhi'a lehua trees are being threatened by a fungus known as Rapid 'Ōhi'a Death or ROD. ROD kills a healthy tree within a few weeks and destroys 10 percent of Hawai'i's 'ōhi'a lehua population annually.

THE INSEPARABLE LOVERS
Inspired by folklore

The goddess of fire Pele strolled across her reclaimed desolate landscape, but an ankle-high scrawny tree with a red spiny blossom defied the jagged lava rock wasteland.

Her heart twinged. She fought back tears.

Wind swayed the scrawny tree's blossoms.

Pele stomped to her Kilauea domain, trying to forget about the lovers, 'Ōhi'a and Lehua.

'Ōhi'a was a handsome warrior, and Lehua was a talented woman. Mortals and gods knew their children were destined for greatness.

But Pele wanted ʻŌhiʻa. She donned her most attractive form and approached when he was alone.

"Aloha," Pele said.

ʻŌhiʻa stepped toward her. "Aloha. I haven't seen you around. What's your name?"

Pele trembled. Her throat constricted. She forced her words through the blockage. "Pele."

Her name lingered in the surrounding trees.

He bowed. "Pelehonuamea. You honor me with your presence."

Pele became light-headed. *He can't be this perfect.* She looked within him. ʻŌhiʻa was flawless. Pele ached for him. "ʻŌhiʻa, you deserve to be with me, a goddess. Not some common girl."

He stepped back and bowed. "Pelehonuamea. You honor me greatly, but Lehua is my love."

Pele's face stung. She rubbed her cheek. The goddess bit her lip to stop the tears blurring her vision. It didn't work. *Anger stops everything.* Pele's eyes flashed. Her sight cleared. "If I can't have you, neither will she."

ʻŌhiʻa ran.

Pele's eyes glowed to summon a lake of lava. But she stopped her conjuring. *No, killing him and destroying their village isn't enough. He'll be a lesson for those who deny me.*

She turned ʻŌhiʻa's body into a scraggly tree trunk. His arms became crooked limbs and his fingers jagged branches. The warrior screamed as his face was petrified.

Pele's tears touched her cheeks and vaporized. "This is how ugly you made me feel." The goddess's glowing eyes dimmed as she stomped to her Kilauea domain.

ʻŌhiʻa's beloved Lehua heard yelling and ran to it. An ugly tree with ʻŌhiʻa's face was in the path.

Lehua's heart sank. Her fingertips brushed the petrified face. "ʻŌhiʻa?"

Yes trembled within Lehua.

Lehua sobbed and wailed against the tree.

Her cries resonated throughout the islands. The gods were moved. They agreed to reunite the lovers but dared not lift Pele's curse.

The deities chanted an incantation that made Lehua a radiant flower and placed her upon 'Ōhi'a's scrawny limb.

To this day, if you pick a lehua blossom, it will rain because the gods weep over the separation of 'Ōhi'a and Lehua.

TEINE SA
SAMOA'S JEALOUS DEMON

T EINE SA ARE THE offspring of a human and god but are neither. They are stunning creatures who attract men they desire and attack women who brush their hair at night, dye it, or wear it down and interact with men the Teine Sa want.

Cursed women and some men experience rapid hair loss, loss of sanity, and death.

Other ways to draw their wrath is to look in a mirror at night. Teine Sa may appear as shadows looming over your reflection's head. To avoid this, cover mirrors at sunset.

Offerings are left where Teine Sa may live. Witnesses passing these places have seen items move or heard their names called. It's customary to say hi and not linger in these areas.

Western missionaries were accused of exploiting the Teine Sa belief to reduce Samoan women's attractiveness.

A TEACHER'S LESSON
Inspired by folklore

A young Caucasian teacher was happy they assigned her to Samoa. After being dropped off at her house, she unbraided her long blond hair and ventured to town.

"Palagi," old Samoan women yelled. "Put up your hair."

She ignored the rude women, purchased some items, and headed home as the sun set.

An older Caucasian teacher greeted her. Her eyes widened. "You wore your hair down in town?"

"Yes, and some rude women harassed me."

"They weren't rude. They were preventing you from attracting a demon."

The young teacher laughed.

"I'm serious. Things are different here. Keep your hair up in public and cover your mirrors at night. That's when the devil uses them."

The young teacher chuckled and went home.

After dinner, she emailed her family and uncovered a mirror.

A shadow loomed over her reflection's head.

THE JEALOUS DEMON
Inspired by folklore

A young Samoan man and woman began a relationship. Their families knew they'd end up together and encouraged them.

The young man headed home from a good day's fishing. While deciding which fish to give his beloved's family, a woman's singing stopped him. He followed the lovely voice to a beautiful woman sitting beneath a palm tree. She brushed her dark hair that covered more of her than her wrap.

She smiled. "You're very handsome."

He went to speak. Air wheezed from his mouth.

She giggled. "Come, sit beside me."

He approached. His fish brushed his leg. His catch was needed for his loved one's dinner.

"The forest is dangerous," his grandmother always said. "Don't talk to women you don't know. They could be Teine Sa."

The beautiful stranger licked her lips. "What's wrong? Don't you like me?"

He lowered his head. "I'm sorry." He ran for his village.

The Teine Sa's eyes narrowed, and she followed him at a distance.

He burst into his house, greeted his family, and handed some fish to his mother.

"Someone's in a rush," she said.

"He wants to see his girlfriend," his younger siblings chanted.

His mother scowled. "Knock it off, or we'll make fun of you when you're older."

His grandmother's gaze burned him. He dashed for the door and stepped outside.

"Wait," his grandmother said.

He and his family froze.

"I want to see you," she said. "And come down here. You're too tall."

The Teine Sa saw him. He kneeled beside his grandmother and her heart fluttered. *He's so respectful.*

His grandmother's wrinkled eyes studied him. "What's wrong?"

He rubbed his clammy hands and resisted looking away.

"Let him go," his mother said. "Her family needs time to prepare the fish."

His grandmother waved him away.

He ran out.

The Teine Sa preened herself.

He called to his beloved.

A young woman ran to him, and they embraced.

The Teine Sa gritted her teeth. Red hue coated her vision as the couple went to a stream. The Teine Sa lurked in the shadows and pulled branches aside to admire her gorgeous man. The girl's laugh was like a baying animal to the Teine Sa.

The couple kissed.

The Teine Sa broke a branch. *I'll possess her tonight when she looks in a mirror and prove how ugly this pathetic child is.*

The couple parted as the sun set.

The Teine Sa followed the young woman home. Her parents were covering mirrors for the night when they greeted her and accepted her boyfriend's fish. She brushed her hair and joined her family for dinner. The Teine Sa giggled as she collected the brushed hair and waited in the mirrors for the girl to uncover one.

The rising sun drove the Teine Sa from the covered mirrors.

Furious that she didn't possess the girl, the entity cursed the collected hair and waited at the palm tree for her gorgeous man.

The young woman became sick and lost some hair.

Her grandmother remembered a childhood neighbor cursed by a Teine Sa lost hair in the same spot.

The young woman's family took her to a healer who cured her.

The couple married and warned their children about the Teine Sa.

KOSCHEI
THE SLAVIC SORCERER

KOSCHEI APPEARS AS A skeletal old man, which could be why his name translates to bone. He has a scraggly beard and a hooked nose but can shape-shift into various creatures or a tornado.

He possesses superhuman strength, stamina, and abducts women to marry.

Koschei is Baba Yaga's male counterpart. They have been depicted as siblings or a married couple. They represent death and the supernatural's dark side.

Killing Koschei involves destroying the needle containing his soul. The needle is in an egg, which is in a duck, in a rabbit, in a chest buried under an oak tree on the invisible island of Buyan. These components are reminiscent of a Russian nesting doll.

Manipulating the egg may control Koschei like a voodoo doll.

KOSCHEI THE IMMORTAL
Inspired by folklore

After a lifetime, Koschei discovered the incantation for immortality. The sorcerer rushed through the dark ritual, and silence fell upon his lair. Then Koschei's soul left his body.

Relishing the sensation, the sorcerer laughed. But haste caused him to miss part of the ritual, and his soul transferred into a needle.

Koschei hid the needle to preserve his immortality and began his dark reign across the lands.

He learned of Princess Marya Morevna's godlike beauty, skill, and grace. Such a woman was worthy of being his wife.

But instead of kidnapping, he sought an audience with her.

From her throne, Marya raised an eyebrow at the unkempt, skeletal man. "Yes?"

He bowed. "Greetings, fair Marya Morevna. I am Koschei, the great—"

"Fiend?" Marya's nails dug into her armrest.

Koschei wheezed a chuckle. "Sorcerer."

"Prove it."

His eyes glowed, and he created a minor illusion.

She smirked.

Koschei's eyes brightened. The illusion grew. His eyes dimmed. "I require some drink."

Marya laughed. "You claim to be the best but tire before I'm impressed? Such a typical man."

Koschei's eyes glowed. A grand spectacle appeared. His eyes dimmed, and he panted. "Now may I have food and drink?"

Marya waved a lazy hand for her attendants to serve him. Her yawn echoed the throne room.

Koschei batted away the refreshments. His eyes glowed, dimmed, and he collapsed.

Marya stood. "Guards, kill him."

They attacked.

Koschei choked a laugh. "Fools, I'm immortal. You cannot kill me."

"Very well, sorcerer," Marya said. "Take him to the dungeon. We'll make torture worse than death."

"I'll have my vengeance," Koschei wheezed. "I'll kill you all." His cackles echoed the castle.

Marya's eyes narrowed. "Refuse him food and water." She stomped to the door. "Ready my horse and greatest detail. There's a way to kill him, and I will find it."

In a castle across the country. Three wizards appeared as an eagle, falcon, and raven to ask Prince Ivan to marry his three sisters.

He accepted their request.

Seasons later, Prince Ivan went to visit his siblings and encountered soldiers beside his river.

"What brings you to my land without proper introductions?"

The soldiers recognized Ivan's insignia and bowed. "Your Majesty. We travel with Princess Marya Morevna and are merely passing through."

Ivan laughed. "You've journeyed to the other side of the world if you speak the truth. Yet you carry her insignia. If you do travel with Marya Morevna, take me to her."

The guards escorted Ivan to Marya.

Her beauty stunned Ivan, and she was taken by him. They talked over meals and discovered they were equal in many traits.

The following day brought a messenger who informed Marya that unrest grew in her neighboring kingdoms.

Ivan ached for Marya as she prepared to leave and proposed to her. She accepted.

Ivan accompanied Marya to her kingdom, and they married.

Tension between neighboring kingdoms demanded Marya's attention, and she readied her detail.

Ivan went to his wife. "I shall go with you."

"Thank you, my love. But if war breaks, I'll need you to secure our kingdom." She kissed him and joined her detail. "You have my trust, my love, and please don't enter the dungeon."

War broke, and Marya joined her allies in battle.

Ivan excelled in running the kingdom but grew curious about the dungeon and peeked inside.

A chained-up, withered old man wheezed in an empty cell, "Is someone there? Please have mercy and bring me water."

Ivan rushed water to him. "Who are you?"

The shriveled man drank like desert sands at midday. "More."

Several buckets later, the man sighed. A wheezing chuckle rumbled from his chest and echoed in the dungeon. "Thank you, boy. I am Koschei."

Ivan paled and fell over the empty bucket.

Koschei's eyes glowed. He broke his chains, became a tornado, and left.

The battlefield was a flurry of clashing weapons and spilled blood. Clouds blackened the noonday sun. Lightning terrified the horses, and rolling thunder stopped the war. A breeze intensified into Koschei's maelstrom. His cackle scattered the armies.

Marya readied her sword to engage him, but the wind took her.

The armies returned to their kingdoms.

Marya's captain of the guards lowered his head to Ivan. "I'm sorry, my lord. Marya is lost. She's was the only one who could best the sorcerer."

"No," Ivan said. "For we are equals." He mounted the kingdom's fastest steed, raced to his three brother-in-law wizards, and asked for help.

The wizards admitted they were no match for Koschei, the immortal, but agreed to help. They gave Ivan a trinket to track the prince and directions to Koschei's castle in the distant lands.

Ivan thanked them and left.

Days later, Ivan shook off the creeping dread as he approached the sorcerer's castle.

Clacking of an approaching horse thundered.

Ivan hid.

A horse carrying Koschei raced from the castle into the wilderness.

Ivan hurried in and found the dungeon containing Marya.

He embraced her. "I'm sorry I didn't listen to you."

She wept against his shoulder. "It's fine, my love. You are doing your best to correct your mistake, but I'm trapped, for Koschei's enchanted steed is the fastest in the land."

"We need to try." Ivan kissed Marya.

They hurried to Ivan's horse and fled.

At a clifftop overlooking the sea, they approached a ramshackle cottage.

Thunder rumbled as Koschei returned to his castle. The sorcerer dismounted, sniffed the air, and faced his horse. "Tell me what's wrong."

The horse's eyes glowed. It faced the dungeon. "Marya is gone." Its nostrils flared. "Prince Ivan rescued her." The horse turned toward the cliffs. "They race for the outskirts."

Koschei cursed and jumped on the horse. "Take me to them."

"Yes, master." The horse leaped into a gallop.

The landscape blurred, and Koschei barreled down upon Ivan and Marya before they passed the ramshackle cottage.

Ivan's horse was startled and threw the couple.

Koschei caught Marya.

Ivan got a face full of dirt and stopped rolling before the cliff.

The surf crashed into rocks below.

Koschei cackled. "You must enjoy visiting dungeons, boy."

Ivan struggled to his feet.

"I applaud your effort and thank you for freeing me. But I'm not as merciful as you." Koschei's eyes glowed. His sword flew into Ivan's chest.

Marya screamed as Ivan fell.

Glowing-eyed Koschei cackled as his flying sword dismembered Ivan. Then the sorcerer sent Ivan's pieces into a barrel beside the cottage, sealed it, and launched it into the sea.

"Enjoy your coffin, Prince Ivan." Koschei cackled and took the sobbing Marya back to his castle.

Ivan's brother-in-law wizards sensed he had died. Using the trinket, they retrieved and restored him.

The wizards bowed. "Please don't be so reckless. We can't revive you again."

Ivan thanked them and returned to Koschei's castle. When the sorcerer thundered into the wilderness, Ivan hurried to the dungeon.

Marya embraced him. "My love. You are not dead."

"My brothers-in-law revived me. But they can't do it again or defeat Koschei. We need to know the source of his power."

"I'll find out tonight. He makes me have dinner with him. Come back after he leaves."

Thunder approached, and the couple parted.

Marya gazed at the feast and smiled at Koschei. "I never realized how powerful my lord is."

He laughed. "It's about time you warmed up to me."

"My lord shouldn't be surprised. You know how fickle women are."

"Quite."

"How did my lord become immortal?"

"I placed my soul in a needle. If it breaks, I die."

"How clever. And where is this needle?"

"I hid it in an egg that's in several animals, in a chest, under a tree on the island of Buyan."

"My lord is so ingenious. How did you enhance your steed?"

"I didn't. I got it from watching Baba Yaga's herd for three days without losing one."

"Baba Yaga's here?"

Koschei laughed. "No, silly child. She's in the thirteenth kingdom. I got there by waving my magic handkerchief at the river of fire."

Marya chuckled. "Magic handkerchief? I think you are making things up."

Koschei's eyes glowed. He produced a handkerchief from the air. It drifted to Marya.

She took it. "My lord is so cunning and well traveled. I wonder, would you know where the sweetest fruit of the land is?"

"Yes. It grows on a tree a year away by horse."

"I'd like to taste such fruit. But it's too far."

"Silly girl. It's a year for mortals but moments for my steed." His eyes glowed. "And seconds if I conjure—"

"Conjure? But can't my lord reach it in moments?"

"Quite." He faded into the shadows and his eyes dimmed.

His steed's thundering hooves raced from the castle.

Prince Ivan entered.

Marya met him in the courtyard, shared what she learned, gave him Koschei's handkerchief and a kiss. "Luck be with you, my love. Now hurry."

Ivan's brothers-in-law gave him directions to the river of fire, a map of the thirteenth kingdom, and how to find Baba Yaga.

At the river of fire, Ivan waved the magic handkerchief. A bridge raised, and he crossed into the mystic realm.

His stomach growled. He caught a bird, but its mother begged Ivan to spare her child for one good deed.

Ivan agreed.

The birds thanked him and flew away.

Ivan captured a lion cub. But its mother begged him to spare her child for one good deed.

Ivan agreed.

The lions thanked him and left.

Ivan found a beehive and was about to destroy it for honey. But the bees begged him to spare their home for one good deed.

Ivan agreed.

The bees thanked him, and Ivan left.

Light from a clearing pierced the dim forest. Glowing skulls on sticks surrounded the chicken-legged house of Baba Yaga.

The door flung open, and the witch's eyes widened. "Prince Ivan? What brings you to my realm?"

"Koschei the sorcerer. He watched your herd for three days and lost none. I wish the same for your fastest steed."

Baba Yaga chuckled. "Very well, Prince Ivan. But if you fail, I get to eat you."

"I agree."

Baba Yaga cackled. "We begin tomorrow. You may sleep on my floor."

The witch's snoring kept Ivan up.

She led him to the stables and leaned into her herd. "All of you scatter. Don't let him catch you, or I'll beat you."

She released the horses, and they scattered.

Bleary-eyed Ivan's jaw dropped.

"I expect them rounded up before I return tonight. Good luck, Prince Ivan." She entered her mortar and flew off, cackling.

The bird Ivan spared and its mother flew to him. "We shall help you, Prince Ivan." They called other birds, and the flock returned the horses.

Ivan thanked them and napped against the stable door.

He woke before Baba Yaga returned.

She swooped from the sky, jumped from her mortar, and screamed, "You horses, why did you return?"

"Birds attacked us."

Baba Yaga sneered. "You better not return tomorrow."

Baba Yaga and Ivan had dinner. The witch slept, but her snoring kept Ivan up.

At daybreak, she led him to the stables, released her horses, and flew away.

But the horses were returned by the lion cub and his mother.

Ivan thanked them, napped beside the stable door, and woke before Baba Yaga returned.

The horrified witch threatened her horses not to return tomorrow.

On the last day, Baba Yaga led tired Ivan to the stables, released her horses, and flew away.

Bees gathered beside Ivan. "We will gather the horses, but Baba Yaga plans to kill you tonight. She's imprisoned the land's fastest stallion at the back of the stables. Stay with it tonight, and both of you leave tomorrow."

Ivan found the stallion lying in the corner.

It tried standing, but its legs trembled, and it stayed down.

Ivan went beside it. "What happened to you?"

"Prince Ivan. Baba Yaga doesn't feed me to keep me from escaping. Why are you here?"

Ivan fed and watered the stallion while telling him about Koschei and Marya.

The stallion nodded. "I'll be strong enough to escape tomorrow but need more time to rescue Marya."

The bees returned the horses. The herd was startled seeing Prince Ivan.

The stallion stood. "Prince Ivan is our guest, which means we'll protect him from Baba Yaga. Understand?"

The horses nodded.

Baba Yaga came home and yelled at the herd for returning.

They made excuses and hid Ivan.

She called for the prince and entered her house.

At dawn, Ivan and the stallion raced for the river of fire. He waved Koschei's handkerchief.

The bridge rose.

"Fools," Baba Yaga echoed above them. "You'll never escape me."

She dove her mortar toward them.

Fire burst from the lake, startling Baba Yaga. Her mortar hit the bridge, and she fell into the fire.

Ivan and the stallion returned to our realm.

In a few days, the stallion was ready. Ivan grabbed his sword, and they went to Koschei's castle.

When the sorcerer thundered from his lair, Ivan entered.

He freed Marya. She embraced him and took a sword. They mounted the stallion. Its eyes glowed, the air trembled, and they raced from the castle.

Koschei sensed the disturbance. He jerked his steed's head. It screamed and halted. The sorcerer forced his horse to return home.

It buckled.

Koschei's heels jabbed the horse. "What's wrong, you miserable animal? Marya is escaping."

"Master, she rides a stallion faster than I."

"I don't care. I'll make you go faster." Koschei hit the steed.

It yelled.

The realm blurred. The sorcerer beat the steed until they barreled down upon the stallion. Marya's hair and dress whipped in the wind, and Ivan glanced back.

The sorcerer smiled. "Prince Ivan, I'll enjoy killing you again." Koschei struck his steed.

The frothing horse screamed, and tears flew from its eyes.

Ivan's stallion's eyes narrowed, and it slowed.

"What are you doing?" Ivan said. "They're almost upon us."

Near the ruined cottage on the cliff, Koschei closed the gap.

The stallion glanced back, then bucked Koschei from his steed and trampled the sorcerer.

Ivan and Marya dismounted with their swords and hacked Koschei.

"Fools, I am immortal. You'll never kill me." He cackled.

Ivan took Marya aside. "He's right."

Koschei's trembling steed approached the stallion. "Thank you, brother."

The stallion nodded.

Marya faced Ivan. "We'll find the needle with his soul and destroy it. But can't risk imprisoning him again."

Ivan nodded and decapitated Koschei.

They hid his head, burned his body, and returned to Marya's kingdom.

Once peace was restored, they departed for the mysterious island of Buyan.

NAMAKA
PELE'S SISTER THE SEA GODDESS

Namaka's full name is Nā-maka-o-Kaha'i which means eyes of Kaha'i. Kaha'i was a Hawaiian demigod.

Namaka controls Hawai'i's harsh ocean currents and waves.

She is Pele's older sister, and while Pele is seen in lava, Namaka appears in the ocean.

When Pele seduced Namaka's husband, the ocean goddess killed Pele's physical form. But Pele became the goddess of fire, allowing her spirit to wander Hawai'i and the sisters to continue their feud.

A SISTER'S WRATH
Inspired by folklore

In the beginning, there was the Pacific Ocean. A canoe broke the horizon. Pele piloted the vessel while her sister, the ocean goddess Namaka, pursued.

Pele, limited in the mystic ways, used borrowed magic to create land.

Namaka formed on the island and loomed over Pele, the woman who seduced her husband. She unleashed her hate on her sister and left Pele's battered body.

But Pele lumbered to her canoe and formed another island to protect her from her sister.

But the island was still too small, and Namaka beat Pele again.

The sisters continued this until Namaka killed Pele.

"Aloha, sister," Namaka said. "I'll tell our parents of your treacherous ways that led to your demise."

Pele's soul flickered.

"No," Namaka whispered.

Pele's soul illuminated the sky. She became the goddess of fire and flew to the island's volcano, Kilauea.

A tear rolled across Namaka's cheek. "Is there no justice?"

THE BEACH STRANGER
Inspired by folklore

Her chores were difficult because of the raging sun. The grass field along her grandmother's property blocked the whispering waves, but their salty breeze graced her sweaty skin and filled her lungs.

Her grandmother, sitting under her shaded porch, fanned herself.

"Tutu," the girl said. "Now can we go to the beach?"

Her grandmother stretched her neck to look over the grass. "No. I don't like how it looks."

The girl frowned and resumed her chores.

The wind stopped.

She sighed and faced her tutu.

The woman's eyes were closed, and her head nodded.

The girl giggled.

Her grandmother's head tilted back, her mouth opened, and she snored.

The youngster snuck to the coconut tree at the edge of the property and ran through the growth. She broke through into the clearing and was welcomed by miles of beach, rolling waves, and blue water that darkened toward the horizon.

Her slippers sank in the sand; the grains burned her feet. She squealed and hurried to the water. On the wet sand, a chill prickled her skin.

A wave crashed, tumbled ashore, and brushed the tip of her slippers.

"Aloha," a woman said behind her.

The girl jumped.

An elderly Hawaiian woman smiled behind her. "I'm sorry. I didn't mean to scare you. It's such a beautiful day. Are you going for a swim?"

I don't remember passing anyone. If she knows my tutu, she'll tell her I'm here and I'll get in trouble. She cried.

"Oh, come here." The Hawaiian woman reached for her.

The child ran back to her tutu. At the tall grass, she looked back.

The woman was gone. But her face was in a wave that crashed against the sand.

Claim your two free stories:

Dr. Glen Grant's Morgan's Corner
Kamuela's Experiences with the Nightmarchers

By joining our email list at:
LegnedsFromThePacific.com/book1-extras

Also By Kamuela Kaneshiro

"Geeky Thriller Series"
I Didn't Mean to Kill My Best Friend
I Didn't Mean to Win the Lottery (web serial)

Academic
The Gangster, The Evolved Detective, and the Dark Knight

Blog Collection
My Sister Monday: A Collection of Science Jokes from the Beloved My Sister Monday Blog
Fun Fact Friday: A Collection of over 150 facts from the Fun Fact Friday Blog

Kickstarter Backers

Mahalo nui loa to the following people who helped make this book possible.

Edward "Pueo" Henke

Lucy Kaneshiro

Warren S. Kaneshiro

***

Crystal Amaya

Arghtwo

Ralph Garcia

Clinton Kaneshiro

Bernard L.

John L.

Bill Medeiros

Ren Shepard

Aaron Toyama

***

Noel Araki

Mama Bon

Keani Kreienbaum

Let's Get Haunted

Nick Lehnert

Mary

Logan M Porter

Leiyomi Preciado

Rebecca

Stephanie

Thomas Umstattd Jr.

Erin Valenciano

***

Max Anderson

Anonymous

Kelly Diana Brogdon

Garon Clements

Amanda Craven

Kristen F.

Miranda Forner

Joanna Gray

Rebekah H.

Wesley Hoffman

Kaas

Marissa Karomfily

Rachel Lulich

Sean M.

Michelle R. Mangio

Rosie Matsumura

John Miyasato

James L. Rubart

Tim Stroup

B. Trammel

***

Bruce Alcorn

Zephyr Barker

Cheyenne Bramwell

Edith F.

Ann G.

Alexandre Gachet

Caitlin H.

Margaret Hamlin

Sergey Kochergan

Jacen Leonard

Mare M.

Danielle Marston

Fay Onyx

Michael "Oz" Orias

John P.

Meagan Rowell

Charlotte Stark

Sarah Swanson

Duane Warnecke

Xtine

If you are a backer, or know a backer who didn't receive their rewards, please contact me at info@legendsfromthepacific.com with your Kickstarter email.

A special mahalo nui loa to our Ukraine supporters.
I hope you, your families, and loved ones are safe.